MISSING ABBY

Also by Lee Weatherly

CHILD X

MISSING ABBY

Lee Weatherly

David Fickling Books

OXFORD · NEW YORK

A DAVID FICKLING BOOK

Published by David Fickling Books
an imprint of Random House Children's Books
a division of Random House, Inc.
New York

Published simultaneously in Canada by Random House of Canada Limited, Toronto.
Originally published in Great Britain by David Fickling Books, an imprint of Random
House Children's Books, in 2004.

www.randomhouse.com/teens

Library of Congress Cataloging-in-Publication Data
Weatherly, Lee.
Missing Abby / by Lee Weatherly.— 1st American ed.
p.   cm.
SUMMARY: As the last one to see thirteen-year-old Abby, Emma is determined to discover
the truth about her mysterious disappearance, spurred in part by her feelings of guilt
over ending their friendship in order to ensure popularity at her new school.
ISBN 0-385-75052-8 (trade)—ISBN 0-385-75053-6 (lib. bdg.)
[1. Missing persons—Fiction. 2. Interpersonal relations—Fiction. 3. Fantasy games—
Fiction. 4. Individuality—Fiction. 5. Schools—Fiction.] I. Title.
PZ7.W3553Mis 2004
[Fic]—dc22
2003026546

Printed in the United States of America
November 2004
10 9 8 7 6 5 4 3 2 1
First American Edition

Acknowledgements

My thanks and gratitude to the following people:

DCI Martin Fotheringham of the Hampshire Constabulary, who generously took the time to answer my questions regarding police procedure. Any mistakes along these lines are solely the fault of the author!

My lovely friend Liz Kessler, for her razor-sharp editorial eye and our inspiring friendship.

Katherine Sunderland and the East Barnet School's Reading and Writing Group, for taking part in reading early drafts of the story – with special thanks to Daniel Bartholomew, Christopher Costigan and Ben Greenbury.

And Ian, Becky, Frances and James, for the use of their cat.

For my husband, Peter – words cannot express

Day One

Missing Person's Report,
Hampshire Constabulary

Date: Sunday 5th September 2004

Full name and address of Missing Person:
Abigail ('Abby') Marie Rypner, 17 Rosemont Street, Garemont, Brookfield, Hants

Age: 13 years, 2 months

Full circumstances of events and details leading up to the report:
Abby was last seen around 10.00 on Saturday, 4th September, when she left the family home on Rosemont Street. She told her mother she was going shopping with friends and then to see a movie in Brookfield. However, her friends claim that she was not due to meet them until that evening (see overleaf for interview details). Abby was expected at her friend Sheila Langley's house around 18.00 that evening, but never arrived. Sheila then rang the Rypner residence at around 19.30, alerting Abby's family. After trying her mobile repeatedly, Abby's family searched the neighbourhood and Brookfield, and finally reported Abby as a MP at 00.16 this morning.

Mental state of the Missing Person, and details of anything that may make them particularly vulnerable:

Mental state normal, so far as her family and friends are aware. MP is considered vulnerable because of her age.

Details of any vehicle used:

MP would have taken the 56 HantsLink Bus service into Brookfield. No other vehicles known at this time.

Full description, including what the Missing Person was last seen wearing:

About 5'5" slight build (approx 8½ stone), long brown hair dyed black. Was wearing black combat trousers, black T-shirt and silver jewellery, and was carrying a rucksack (contents unknown)

Based on interviews, possible reasons/speculation why this person may have disappeared:

None known.

Police Constable taking report: Elizabeth Lavine

Day Two

THE FORCE IS STRONG IN THIS ONE

I was already lying awake, but I still started like I had been cattle-prodded when Darth bellowed at me. He does that to me every morning, even if he is only nine inches tall and plastic. *GET UP AND FIGHT LIKE A JEDI*, he breathed, waving a glowing light sabre.

'You are *so* predictable. It's just sad.' I pushed the button beside Darth's foot.

A knock rapped on my door. 'Emma!' called Jenny. The door opened, and my stepmother peered around it. She almost looks like a kid herself, with her freckles and tumble of brown hair. 'Hey, well done you! Thought you might have overslept.'

'On the first day of Year Nine? You're mad!'

I hummed as I pulled on my green uniform. Normally I completely loathe uniforms, but I have to admit that I sort of like the ones we have at St Seb's – crisp and dark green, like a school full of forest sprites. I shook my head. Note to self: do not share that thought with Jo and Debbie; they'll think you're demented.

I looked in the mirror as I brushed my hair, admiring how the light caught its new tints. My hair used to be boring brown, like my eyes, but I'd had gold and auburn streaks added to it the week before (ignoring Dad's predictable moaning). And the difference was *amazing*. I actually looked halfway interesting for a change.

A quick touch of mascara – which, contrary to what our form head would have you believe, you *can* get away with – and I was done. I smiled at myself in the mirror. This year was going to be the best ever, I just knew it. Last year I had been the new girl, but now I had Jo and Debbie for friends. People actually liked me, knew who I was. I still couldn't get used to it.

My smile faded as I saw myself being slammed against a wall, books flying. A chorus of shrieking laughter: 'Hey freak, you've dropped something – clumsy cow!'

Ancient history; nothing to do with me any more. Taking a deep breath, I twisted the top back onto the mascara. Popping it into my handbag, I snapped it shut with a sharp *click*.

I had put Balden Comp completely behind me. And that's where it was going to stay.

By the time I slid into my place at the kitchen table, my six-year-old half-sister Nat was already there, grimly mashing a banana into a bowl of cereal. The ribbon on one of her thick plaits was coming undone already. Nat's hair is like this thing in science called chaos theory.

'Can I tempt you, Emma?' Jenny was grilling bacon. I don't know how she stays so thin when she has a bacon sandwich every morning for breakfast.

'Just tea for me, thanks. Here, I'll get it.' I jumped up from the table. Watching Nat assault the banana was making me feel seriously ill.

'Oh, have some toast, too – live it up.' Jenny glanced over her shoulder. 'Natalie, just eat your breakfast, don't play with it.'

Nat heaved a sigh like this was just too much to ask, and let her spoon drop with a clatter. 'Emma, can we play a game?'

'Not *now*! I've got to go to school.'

'So do you, Natalie,' pointed out Jenny. She poked at the bacon with a fork, flipping it over.

'No, I want to play with Emma! *Please*, Emma? Please please please?' She clasped her hands under her chin, like a music-hall heroine begging for mercy.

'Maybe later.' I poured boiling water from the kettle over a tea bag. Yeah, maybe. If Jo and Debbie were nowhere to be seen. I'd *die* if they knew about the babyish games I played with Nat. Definitely weird, to enjoy hanging out with a six-year-old.

'Fine, I'll go watch TV, then!' Nat flounced away from the table and ran into the lounge. Jenny started to stop her, and then shrugged as the sound of the TV drifted in.

'Never mind, we can have our breakfast in peace, can't we? Or until the next catastrophe, at least.'

We sat down at the table. I had to shove a pile of books and papers out of my way, because Jenny uses the kitchen table as a desk during the day. She wants to be a child psychologist, so she started taking classes at the local tech college last year, to get the qualifications she's missing. Which gave Dad a bit of a shock, but Jenny's completely determined. I think it's great – I wouldn't want to sit at home all day polishing the furniture, either.

I spread marmalade on my toast, licking a bit off my fingers as I glanced at her textbooks. A-level psychology and GCSE maths.

Jenny grimaced. 'I put the maths off for as long as I could, but I have to do it now . . . I'm worried about it already; I have to get at least a C grade.'

I bit into my toast. 'You'll get it.'

'I'll have to ask Tom for help.' She made a face, scraping her curly hair back. 'Never mind – thick as a brick, me, but I'll get there eventually. Even if it takes me ten years to get to uni.'

'*Jen*-ny, you're not thick!'

'At maths, my dear, I am definitely thick.'

Silence draped over us as Jenny started reading the *Daily Post*. I sat eating my toast, lost in a marvellous daydream of what this year would be like. Jo and Debbie and I, striding down the corridors with our arms linked, laughing . . . Smiling to myself, I reached for another of the golden triangles in the toast rack.

That's when I saw the headline on the folded-back bit of Jenny's newspaper.

'Oh, my god!' I gasped.

'What?' Jenny lowered her newspaper to look at me.

'No! Give me your paper!' I jumped out of my chair and grabbed at it, flipping it over. The headline said, HAMPSHIRE TEENAGER REPORTED MISSING. And there was a photo of Abby.

Jenny's hand flew to her mouth. 'It's that girl you used to know, isn't it?'

I didn't bother answering her. I was too busy gulping down the story in short, terrible bursts.

Abigail Ryzner, 13, was reported missing by her parents late Saturday evening . . . She had said she was going shopping in Brookfield and later to a friend's house, but CCTV footage of the town centre has so far failed to corroborate this . . . she never arrived at the friend's house, and has apparently not been seen by anyone since around ten o'clock on Saturday . . . witnesses who saw Abby that day are urged to come forward . . .

'Oh, Emma! Oh, I hope she's all right.' Jenny had been reading over my shoulder, and now she sank back into her seat, her face pale. 'She lives over by your old house, doesn't she? I remember seeing you with her a few times, when Tom and I used to pick you up for weekend visits. Oh, her poor parents . . .'

The realization hit me like a lorry-load of concrete. 'But Jenny, *I* saw her!'

My stepmother's gaze sharpened. 'What do you mean? In town?'

'No – no, I saw her, on the bus, on Saturday! We were coming home from town at the same time – we sat together, we talked—'

'When was this?'

'Around – I don't know, about one o'clock or so. Because you and I were going swimming at two, remember?'

My gaze fell to the paper again. *Not been seen by anyone since ten o'clock on Saturday . . .* Oh my god, was

13

I the last person to have seen her, then? I *couldn't* have been!

A sick lump rose in my throat, and I started to babble helplessly: 'But – but we sat and talked – I mean, what could have happened to her? She must be OK, don't you think? I mean, she was fine, there wasn't anything wrong—'

'I don't know, love.' Jenny squeezed my shoulder as she rose and crossed quickly to the kitchen phone, her slippered feet padding on the floor. She picked up the receiver and started to dial.

'What are you doing?' I asked, staring at her.

'Calling the police, of course.'

When I had spotted Abby at the town centre bus stop that afternoon, my first thought had been, *Oh, no! Hide!*

She was looking even stranger than usual, dressed in black combat trousers and a black T-shirt with a screaming green skull on it. Dozens of slithery silver chains hung around her neck, like metallic snake-skin. She stood leaning against the bus shelter, reading a paperback with a dragon on the cover. Even from where I was standing, I could see that her nails were long and pointy, painted black.

God, not her!

I started to duck back behind the corner of the bus station, but a sudden flare of anger stopped me. Why should I be stopped from going home just because of Abby? The next bus wasn't for half an hour; I'd be late if I didn't catch this one!

What was she going to do, bite me?

Mind you, she looked a bit vampireish these days.

Abby solved the problem by glancing up and seeing me. At first she looked stunned, and then she smiled uncertainly. 'Emma . . . ! How are you doing?'

Trapped. Slowly, I crossed the few steps to the bus stop, trying to smile. 'I'm OK. How about you?'

'All right.' She turned down the corner of the page she had been reading, and stuffed the book into the battered grey rucksack that sat by her feet. She looked up at me as she zipped it, tucking a strand of long dark hair behind her ear. 'I haven't seen you for ages.'

Her eyes lingered on the bright embroidery that swirled up the legs of my jeans. My face felt hot as I remembered how she used to laugh at what she called the fashion clones.

That was a lifetime ago! But I couldn't quite meet her gaze as I flipped my hair back, scaldingly conscious of its glimmering new tints. 'Um, yeah, it's been a while. How are things at Balden?'

She shrugged, standing up. I could hardly even see her eyes, with the amount of black eyeliner she had on. 'Same ol', same ol' . . . the teachers are all idiots, as usual. How's life at the wonderfully-rated St Seb's?'

'Oh – great.' My flush deepened.

The bus came just then, lumbering into the station like a prehistoric beast. We shuffled along in the queue together, surrounded by Saturday shoppers clutching plastic bags.

'How's your mum doing?' The bright sunlight showed the green flecks in Abby's eyes. 'Does she like it in America?'

Thank god, a neutral topic! 'Yeah, she loves it. I spent three weeks in Chicago with her last month.'

Mum remarried a couple of years ago, to this bloke called Paul. He's OK, I guess. Except that right after they got married, he got this offer to go work in Chicago for three years. Mum kept talking about what a *fantastic opportunity* it was for me, so she was a bit narked when I told her I didn't want to go. Then there was this big conference with her, Dad and Jenny, and the upshot of it was that Mum would have the fantastic opportunity on her own, and that I'd live with Dad and Jenny for three years.

Weird as it was to think about now, I had actually been sort of gutted to move into Dad's house when Mum left – because it had meant not living across the street from Abby any more.

We showed our passes to the driver. Abby took a seat about halfway back, shoving her rucksack down by her feet. And I couldn't keep walking down the aisle and sit somewhere else; it would be too rude, too obvious. I sank down beside her, willing the journey to go faster than usual.

The bus lurched away from the stop. It felt like a sauna on wheels. How could Abby bear to wear black in this heat? Well, I suppose the Goth Fashion League would kick her out if she wore anything else.

Guilt pierced me. This was *Abby,* even if we weren't friends any more. I took a breath and smiled at her. 'Um, how are Greg and Matthew?'

She grimaced, wrinkling the spray of freckles across her nose. 'Little terrors . . . they get worse all the time.' She glanced at me, and something like her old mischievous expression played about her mouth. 'Remember all the wars we used to have?'

A flash of memory hit me, and I snorted softly, smiling. 'Yeah . . . like the time Matthew got hold of Sparkles. I was ready to kill him.'

'Oh, yeah! I had forgotten all about Sparkles. And I had Zeus, didn't I?' Abby deepened her voice: 'Fly away to the crimson forest! Away!'

I almost laughed as it all came back. Playing My Pretty Ponies with Abby had been like playing it with no one else in the world. I bet no one else's green pony turned evil and would have destroyed all ponykind, if we hadn't captured it and put it through elaborate healing rituals. We played that game, in instalments, for the better part of the whole year that we were nine.

Freak. The word slithered into my mind, breaking the spell.

There was an awkward silence. I shifted on my seat, praying for the bus to go faster.

Suddenly Abby leaned over to root about in her rucksack. 'Here, look at this,' she said, prying open a long, white box.

There was a chunky gold necklace inside, made up of golden-striped stones. Completely gaudy, but beautiful in a way, like a garish sunset. Just the sort of thing we would have loved to pretend was magic when we were about ten.

'Isn't it great?' Abby turned the box from side to side.

'Yeah, fantastic.' I looked away, wondering whether she was *allergic* to normality, or what.

'They're called tigers' eyes – they're supposed to symbolize courage.' Abby tried to get the box into her backpack again. As she shoved aside a two-litre bottle of Pepsi, I saw a sleek blue and gold book with *Monster Manual* on the cover.

Abby grinned. 'Don't worry, I haven't started keeping gargoyles in the back garden. It's for Dungeons and Dragons. I play with some friends of mine.'

She pulled the book out and leafed through it. Drawings of bizarre creatures, with descriptions about each one. *Troglodyte. Yellow Musk Creeper and Zombie.*

I stared at the book as the creatures flipped past. The artwork on its glossy pages was incredible.

Abby's brown eyes glinted at me. 'You've heard of Dungeons and Dragons, right? D&D?'

'Ah – no, actually.' I looked away from the book, picking at a bit of embroidery on my jeans. But her voice just kept enthusing on, not noticing that I wasn't exactly enthralled.

'Oh Emma, you'd love it! See, you invent a character that you play, and then a Games Master takes you through a pretend world – it's fantastic! I'm just about to start GM-ing myself, actually; I've written the story and everything.'

My shoulders tensed. She hadn't changed at all, then, with her weirdness and imaginary games! God, I was *so* glad I'd left Balden.

Abby turned a page. 'Usually you play it sitting around a table, but that's kind of boring, compared to the great stuff you and I used to do.'

'Mmm, yeah.' I stared out the front window. Almost there, almost there.

'So I'm about to get my group into live action gaming instead . . . not that they realize it yet.' She glanced at me almost shyly, playing with one of her silver chains. 'Um . . . you know, you could play with us, if you wanted to. I bet you'd love it.'

I couldn't *believe* she was suggesting this. I'd have to be frothing-at-the-mouth mad to get involved with her again, after everything that happened at Balden!

'Great,' I said tightly.

'We're playing tonight, if—'

Oh, *god,* no! 'No, um – Dad wants me home for this sort of . . . dinner thing.'

'Well . . . what about coming along with me this afternoon, then? That should be almost as much fun. Remember the Esmerelda game? It's sort of like that, but even better.'

I felt hot and cold at the same time. 'Sorry, but Jenny and I are going swimming.'

There was a long, stiffening pause. Finally Abby clapped the book shut, shoving it back into the rucksack. 'Oh, right. Well, *that* sounds interesting. Never mind, then.'

'Maybe sometime . . .' I said, and then wanted to tie and gag myself.

'Yeah, that's OK.'

'I'll, um, ring you,' I heard myself mutter.

Her dark eyes met mine steadily. 'Right.' And it was obvious that she was saying, *We both know you won't, so why bother lying about it?*

I let out a breath, looking away. How awkward could something get before you just *died*?

The next stop was mine. I leapt up like a Jack-in-the-box, grabbing my stuff. 'Well, I've got to go . . . see you.'

Abby propped a knee to her chest, looping her arms around it as she looked out the window. 'Yeah, see you.'

'Bye.' I tried not to seem like I was in a hurry, but I stumbled as I made my way down the aisle, knocking my shopping bag against the other seats. 'Sorry,' I muttered to an old lady with blue-rinsed hair.

'Hey, Emma . . .' called Abby.

What now? I winced and turned around. She smiled at me, but it didn't reach her eyes.

'You know, you'd really love D&D . . . or at least, the *old* you would have.'

'Right,' I said. And I scarpered off the bus as fast as I could, bursting into the September sunshine like an escaped prisoner.

I sat moulded to the kitchen chair while Jenny spoke to the police. 'My stepdaughter, Emma Townsend . . . yes, that's right, she says she saw her Saturday afternoon, around one o'clock . . .'

In the front room I could hear the TV going, and Nat murmuring to herself as she played some sort of game. It all sounded unreal, like noises beaming down from Jupiter.

Finally, Jenny hung up the phone.

'What did they say?'

She turned the kettle on, looking a bit pale. 'They're going to come talk to you at school this morning.'

'At school? But—' I bit off the rest of my protest as about a dozen different emotions swept over me. Fear of what had happened to Abby, *anger* at Abby for running away or whatever she had done, ruining my first day back – sudden terror that she had done it because of me, because I had hurt her feelings so badly on the bus . . .

'Are you all right, Emma?' Suddenly Jenny was at my side. She handed me a fresh cup of tea. 'Here, drink this, love.'

I looked at the clock. 'I'm – I'm going to be late.'

'I'll drive you. I have to take Natalie to school anyway.'

I drank the tea, feeling cold, and wondered what Jo and Debbie would say when police officers turned up at school to talk to me.

'Ems, look at your *hair*! You look fantastic!' cried Jo when I walked into school. She and Debbie were waiting for me by the trophy cases in the foyer, as usual. Jo was almost as tall as me, with sleek blond hair and a wide smile, and Debbie was just the opposite – small and dramatic-looking, with wavy dark hair and big eyes.

I rushed over to them, and we all hugged. We had zapped texts and e-mails back and forth all summer, but it had been weeks since I had seen either of them.

Jo had been visiting her aunt in Shropshire, and Debbie's family had been away on holiday.

'It looks great!' breathed Debbie, touching an auburn-tinted strand on my shoulder. '*Very* sultry. Did you get it done in Chicago?'

'No, here.'

'But I thought your dad—'

I managed a grin. 'Jenny and I ganged up on him, and he caved in eventually.'

'You look *so* sophisticated . . . what kind of tints could I get done, do you reckon?' Jo flipped up a strand of her own hair, grimacing at it.

'Don't be daft, yours is perfect the way it is! Mine needed a lift – oh-so-boring brown isn't exactly a fashion statement.'

Jo and Debbie laughed, and a feeling of confusion rushed over me. What was I *doing*, babbling away about fashion statements? I opened my mouth to tell them about Abby . . . and then shut it again. I didn't know where to start.

The first bell split the air, saving me.

'Right, where do we go, then?' Jo fished her schedule out of her bag.

'English block, room 12A,' said Debbie, reading over her shoulder. 'Mrs Conway – excellent!'

We grabbed our bags and started heading towards our new form room, jostled in the stream of green uniforms.

'Right, Ems, tell us about Chicago!' Debbie walked like a dancer, light and bouncing on her toes. 'You're *so* lucky. My family just went to France again – this completely lobotomised village where the most exciting thing is the bread van coming around twice a week.'

'Oh, can't we hear about that instead?' Jo's mouth was solemn. 'It sounds really educational.'

'It's boring enough to be educational. Come on, Ems, entrance us.'

'Yeah, let us live vicariously through you.' Jo bumped me with her arm.

'Um . . .' My hand tightened on the strap of my bag. It felt like I was travelling further and further from being able to tell them about Abby. But – oh, so what? She was probably safe and sound at home by now! Probably the police wouldn't even turn up.

We got to the English block, and leaned against the wall with the others while we waited for Mrs Conway to open the door.

'Ems . . .' whined Debbie. '*Talk.*'

I shoved Abby away. 'Well, it was completely amazing. Mum works at this gallery near the lake, and we went to all these really arty shops shops there – you know, places where you stare at everything and think yes, it's nice, but what is it? Then we did the tourist thing and went up the Sears Tower – it's wild; it's so high that you feel dizzy just going up the lift . . .'

I didn't mention the other stuff that had struck me – like the way the lake looked like a cold, exotic sea, so that you could almost imagine a Viking ship cresting over the horizon, or the way the wind howled around the skyscrapers. I had learned a thing or two at Balden.

'It sounds fantastic!' breathed Jo. 'All those shops!'

I flipped my hair back. 'I know! Oh, and then Paul, that's my stepfather, took us to a Cubs game. Baseball is *completely* mandatory in Chicago. Paul says if you don't go to the games, they tar and feather you and throw you over the border into Canada . . .'

My voice faded away as I saw Mrs Gates from the office hustling towards us, plump and determined-looking.

'Emma, you're to come to Mrs Ottawa's office immediately.'

Mrs Gates kept giving me strange looks over her glasses as we walked down the empty corridor. Suddenly I realized that she thought the police were there for *me*. Like I had been stealing cars or something.

A wild urge to giggle swept over me. But then we got to Mrs Ottawa's office, and the laugh died in my throat.

Mrs Gates knocked, opening the door. 'Here's Emma.'

The headmistress stood up from behind her desk and came over to me, beckoning with her hand. 'Emma, good. Come in, dear.'

Mrs Gates shut the door behind her, giving me a final hard stare.

I could see the police constables, a man and a woman, sitting in a pair of office chairs in a blaze of white and black. I swallowed, suddenly feeling as guilty as if I *had* been stealing cars.

'Here, Emma, have a seat.' Mrs Ottawa steered me

to a chair. 'This is PC Lavine and PC Morton. They just need to ask you some questions – nothing to be afraid of.' She nodded encouragingly at me as she sat back down, her round face kind.

'I'm PC Lavine, Emma,' said the woman, smiling at me.

I tried to smile back, shifting on the uncomfortable plastic seat. I was surprised at how pretty she was – she had soft milk-chocolate skin, and sleek black hair. She even wore lipstick.

'We understand that you saw Abby Ryzner on Saturday, is that right?'

'Yes, um – we were on the bus together, coming home from town.' I rubbed my palms on my skirt.

'Are you sure it was Abby?' asked PC Morton. He was about Dad's age, with receding blond hair and a bit of a paunch. He flipped open a notebook and scribbled something down, just like on TV.

'Yes, I'm positive. We – used to be friends. I mean, we used to go to school together . . . anyway, we sat together and talked. I'm totally positive.'

'What time was this?' asked PC Lavine. Beside her, PC Morton's pen was scratching away non-stop.

I watched it move across the page like I was hypnotized. 'About one o'clock.'

'Which bus?'

'The number 56 – the one that goes past Garemont Estate. That's where Abby and I both used to get off when I lived there, but now I get off before then, at Larkwood.'

PC Morton looked up. 'OK, Emma, I'd like you

to just tell us everything that happened. What did Abby say when you spoke to her? Did she seem strange at all?'

No stranger than usual popped into my mind.

'Um . . . well, she was talking about Dungeons and Dragons, this game she was playing with her friends . . . and she said it had been sort of boring, the way they had been playing, and that she was going to start a new sort of game herself, or something . . . oh, and she mentioned this game that the – that the two of us used to play, called the Esmerelda game . . .' I trailed off, twisting the sleeve of my blazer.

'What was that?' asked PC Morton.

My skin prickled hotly. 'Nothing! It was just . . . stupid. We pretended to be novice sorcerers, and we had to defeat this evil enchantress called Esmerelda. I mean, it was years ago; it was just a pretend game.'

The questioning went on for ages, over an hour. They were really nice about it – especially PC Lavine, who had sympathetic dark eyes that seemed to understand everything I said – but it just went on and on. They asked practically everything you could imagine, and then asked it all again in slightly different ways, urging me to remember everything I could.

It wasn't easy, since I had tried so hard *not* to listen to Abby at the time. Plus I was so nervous I could hardly remember my own name.

Finally, at the end, I took a breath. 'When I got off the bus, she was sort of – angry at me, I guess.'

'Angry how?' asked PC Lavine.

'Well, she – she made a sort of snide comment

about the "old me". You don't think that she ran away because of *that*, do you? Because I wouldn't go with her that afternoon?'

PC Morton glanced up sharply from his notepad. 'Do you think she ran away, then? Did she say or do anything to give you that impression?'

'No, but – well, what else could it be?' I stared at him in bewilderment, and saw a small, sad smile cross his face. He flipped his notebook shut and stood up. PC Lavine did too, reaching for her hat.

'Emma, thank you; you've been most helpful. Let us know if you remember anything else . . . we'll be back in touch if we have any other questions.'

It's not every day that the police turn up at St Sebastian's. Jo and Debbie were *agog* when I slipped into Maths twenty minutes late, after missing English altogether. As I handed Mrs Bienvenuto my late pass, I saw that they had snagged a table near the back, and were saving a seat for me. Jo waved at me, motioning to the empty seat beside her.

'I think your friends would like for you to sit with them,' said Mrs Bienvenuto dryly, peering at them. Jo grinned back at her, unabashed. 'Well, go on, then. We're all waiting.'

I hurried to the table in the back, feeling everyone's stares on me.

'You were gone *hours!*' whispered Debbie when I sat down. Her small, vivid face was all eyes. 'What happened? Was that police car here because of you?'

'Um – yeah, I suppose.' I fumbled through my textbook with cold fingers. All I wanted to do was put my head down on the desk and cry. Except that I was *not* someone who burst into tears during class any more.

'*Ems* . . . what's going on?' Jo's usually the calm one, but for once she looked as wound up as Debbie.

Taking a breath, I glanced at the front of the room. '. . . So, if our imaginary firm's profits rose by fifteen percent to seventy-two thousand pounds . . .' Mrs Bienvenuto was entranced with the figures on the whiteboard, not looking at us.

I flipped to a fresh page in my notebook and wrote, *This girl from my old school has gone missing, and I was the last person to see her on Saturday. We were on the bus together, coming home from town.*

'Oh, my god,' whispered Debbie. 'What's happened to her, do you think?'

'I don't know,' I whispered back. 'She didn't seem like she was running away or anything—'

I suddenly realized that the class had gone silent. Mrs Bienvenuto stood drumming her fingers on her desk. 'If you're *quite* finished talking, Emma, may I continue with my lesson?'

'Yes, miss.'

'You're sure, now?' There were a few snickers.

'Yes, completely.'

'Oh, good.' She turned back to the whiteboard.

'Later, OK?' whispered Debbie, and I nodded. Then I spent the rest of the lesson staring down at my textbook, trying to figure out how I could tell them about Abby without mentioning what had happened at Balden.

After school that afternoon, I curled up on the settee watching the soaps. Nice safe pretend worlds. Pippin, our ancient ginger cat, jumped creakily into my lap and curled up. I stroked him, grateful for his warmth – even though he drools a bit, and leaves a blanket of orange hairs attached to everything he touches.

'You're a good cat,' I whispered, scratching him behind the ears. He kneaded my leg with his paws, humming deliriously to himself. At least someone was happy.

Around six o'clock, I heard Dad come home, and low murmurs drifted out from the kitchen. Jenny, filling him in on what had happened. My muscles tightened as I strained to listen.

Suddenly my attention jerked back to the TV set, and I sucked in my breath.

Abby was on the news.

I watched, sickly mesmerized, as they showed what looked like a recent home video of Abby and her two brothers messing around in the Ryzner's overgrown back garden.

'. . . the Brookfield teenager, who has been missing since Saturday afternoon. Hampshire Police have launched an intensive investigation to find Abby . . .'

On the video, there was a barbecue going, and Abby pointed at it dramatically, laughing. She had on her black combats again, and a T-shirt with an elaborate Celtic design.

The home video vanished, and a newsreader gazed out solemnly from the screen. 'Today an old school friend reported seeing Abby on a bus, just after one o'clock on Saturday. But the Hampshire teenager never reached home, although the bus stop was less than a five minute walk from her house.'

Suddenly Mr and Mrs Ryzner were on the screen, perched on the beige settee in their living room. Shock rocked through me at the sight of Abby's mum. Mrs Ryzner was always so elegant – and now she just looked old and tired, with a sagging face and her hair scraped back in a ponytail.

'Abby, if you've run away, please come home. We won't be angry, love, we promise.'

Mr Ryzner's arm tightened around her shoulders. He had dark bruises under both eyes. 'Please, Abby, if you're watching this – just come home, and whatever the problem is, we'll work it out.'

The smooth-voiced newscaster came on again. 'Police have not ruled out the possibility of foul play in Abby's disappearance, and are urgently appealing for any witnesses who –'

Suddenly I couldn't take it any more, and I lunged for the remote, switching the TV off. Then I started as Dad sat down on the sofa beside me. I hadn't even known he was in the room.

'Hang on, love—' He switched the TV on again. But the news had gone on to something else by then, thank god. He turned the volume down, and put his arm around me.

'Jenny told me what happened. Are you OK?'

'Dad, do you think she's all right? I mean, they said – they said there might have been foul play.' The words sounded grim, archaic.

'I don't know, love. I wish I did.'

I stared at him, and then looked quickly away, my fingers knotting together. I couldn't bear to think of it. I just couldn't.

He let out a breath, rubbing his chin. 'Jenny's going to ring her parents, see if there's anything we can do . . . I can't even imagine what they must be going through.'

Jenny hardly knows the Ryzners – trust Dad to get out of doing that sort of thing! Actually, I realized suddenly, *I* should be the one to ring them, not Dad or Jenny.

Except for one tiny problem: they probably hated me.

Dad shook his head, pulling his tie free of his shirt and dropping it on the cushion beside him. His temples were frosted with grey, like someone had swiped a paintbrush over his dark hair. 'It sounds terrible, but I have to say I'm glad you aren't friends with Abby any more.'

I stiffened. 'What do you mean?'

He settled back against the sofa, frowning at the TV. 'Well, who can say whether it was a factor or not, but she does seem to have gone off the rails a bit. Only ever wearing black, and all that spooky make-up. God only knows what sort of people she was hanging around with. They could have been into drugs, or worse.'

Abby, doing drugs? She was completely manic on the subject; drugs were for losers and wasters.

'You're wrong. She wouldn't do that.' My voice shook.

'Well, maybe not.' Dad didn't look convinced.

Nat had edged into the room at some point, watching us with wide, steady eyes. 'Mummy said that you're very sad right now, and I'm not to disturb you,' she announced.

'Oh.' My arms seemed to cross over my chest of their own accord. On TV, a woman was holding up a packet of loo roll like it was a gold trophy.

Nat looked down, dragging an exaggerated toe across the carpet. She looked like a miniature sailor in her blue and white school uniform. 'And she said I shouldn't remind you about playing with me today. Like you said we'd do.'

I almost laughed. She was *so* obvious.

'Not today, Nat,' said Dad. 'Maybe Emma will feel like playing with you tomorrow.'

Nat's lower lip considered sulking, and then she changed her mind and came closer, leaning against the sofa and peering up into my face. 'Why are you sad?'

'Because . . .' I shook my head.

'She's worried about a friend of hers,' said Dad. 'But don't pester her about it, OK?'

'But I want to know why—'

Dad leapt off the sofa suddenly, scattering cushions. 'I feel . . . a tickle attack coming on!'

'No-o!' squealed Nat, her face bursting in glee as

Dad scooped her up. He swung her upside down, his hands like busy spiders. She screamed with laughter, kicking her legs.

Finally Dad dropped her onto the big leather chair, where she lay convulsing with giggles. His arms hung down by his sides as he turned and looked at me. 'Are you all right, love? If you want to talk . . .'

Have a word with Jenny, I finished in my mind. 'I'm fine,' I said, staring at the TV.

I couldn't sleep that night, and finally around midnight, I sat up in bed and opened my window. Propping my chin on my hand, I breathed in the smells from the garden. And all at once I was back with Abby, on a summer night over two years ago – the two of us lying on a blanket in her back garden, staring up at the stars.

Do you think there's life on other planets?

Sure, why not? Little purple men with buggy eyes, buzzing around in spaceships, doing crop circles for a laugh . . .

Yeah, really! 'What shall we do this time, Zeebor? How about a giant smiley face?'

'No, we did that last week. Ooh, I know – we'll do lots of circles, like we're saying something profound about infinity, har har har! That'll get 'em going!'

Anyway, come on, seriously . . . what do you think?

God, I don't know . . . yeah, I guess. I mean, look at all those stars . . . we couldn't just be alone, could we?

My hand grew numb with my chin resting on it. I folded my arms and dropped my head on them. Abby and I could always talk like that to each other – saying absolutely anything that came to mind, without having to stop and worry about whether it fitted in, or sounded stupid.

But I guess that's just something you have when you're younger, isn't it? It's not the real world. I mean, it's not something that you can keep once you start to get older, and things start to change. You can't stay that vulnerable and wide-eyed forever, not without getting your teeth kicked in.

I guess I should be grateful to Karen Stipp and the rest of them at Balden, for teaching me that. Year Seven in a new school; it was supposed to be so great. I rubbed my temple, remembering the time she and her cronies had cornered me in the girls' loo.

Hey, Freaky, we saw you and Goth-geek playing one of your little magic games today! Can we play?

We were not! We were just talking—

Oh, you're such a liar! You were playing at magic-wagic, *we saw you! C'mon, Freak – let's play the* magic-wagic *game. It's easy – I do this, and poof, you vanish!*

She had shoved me against the wall, and I'd slipped and fallen, banging my head against a sink. The other two – Amy and Claire – took off then, laughing hysterically as they shoved out the door. Karen stayed behind long enough to actually help me up. She smiled sweetly into my face, tossing her golden-brown hair.

You should be more careful, Freaky – you're always so clumsy! I wouldn't tell anyone about how clumsy you are, if I were you. You know what would happen, right? Still smiling, she pinched my arm, twisting the skin with her long nails until I yelped.

When Dad asked about my bruises, I spun him a tale about falling during PE, playing netball. I wasn't about to tell him the truth – that his daughter was a *freak* who everyone hated. It's not exactly the sort of news flash you want to give your dad, is it?

I shut my window and lay down again, staring up at the ceiling.

I don't know why that time came to mind just then, out of all the dozens of times with Karen. It wasn't like it was even the worst one, not by a long shot.

The girls' changing rooms flashed into my mind, and I shivered.

Day Three

'Hampshire schoolgirl Abby Ryzner is still missing. The
CID has been brought in to head up investigations, and
to aid Hampshire police with the overwhelming number
of phone calls and tips that have been pouring in,
though as yet detectives say they have received little
of interest to them . . .'

Local news broadcast, Tuesday, 7th September.

I overslept that morning, and rushed into class just
after the last bell. Mrs Conway was already taking the
register, her limp blond hair looking defeated.

'Sorry I'm late, miss.'

'That's all right, Emma, just don't make a habit
of it . . .' Mrs Conway lifted her voice above everyone's
talking. 'David Cianci? Ah, there you are. *Please* stop
talking, you lot, or just keep it down, at least . . .'

Jo and Debbie were sitting at a table by the window.
I had managed to put them off yesterday, but now they
started pelting me with questions the moment I sat down.

'I saw it on the news last night, about that girl who
went missing!'

'Yeah, Abby Ryzner – what do you think *happened* to her?'

'She went to Balden Comp, right?'

Like torpedoes, one after another. I grabbed the easiest one first. 'Yeah, she went to Balden. I mean, she *goes* to Balden.'

'Oh, yeah, of course.' Jo paused, her mouth pursing worriedly. 'I just meant – well, you know. It's all sort of scary, isn't it?'

'Yeah, really,' said Debbie. 'She just stepped off the bus and hasn't been seen since . . .' She shook her head, looking a bit awed, but there was also a glimmer of excitement or drama or whatever in her eyes. In Jo's, too, come to that.

'Anyway, so you went to Balden together before you came here?'

'How well did you know her?'

'I – well, actually, we were friends,' I admitted.

Their mouths dropped open in unison. 'Oh, no!' gasped Debbie.

'Oh, *Ems* . . .'

'No, I mean . . . we're not friends *now*. We haven't been friends for ages.'

'But still, you must feel awful!' said Debbie.

'Were you really good friends?' Jo's eyes were wide and worried.

I lifted a shoulder, trying to look offhand, like it had all happened a million years ago. 'Yeah, um – I guess we used to be.'

'What *happened*? I mean—' Debbie stopped awkwardly, a flush staining her cheeks.

38

Jo squeezed my arm. 'Ems, you don't have to tell us! Only if you want to.'

I did have to, though. Or at least, I had to tell them *something*. I took a breath. It was like picking my way through a minefield.

'Well, we were really good friends in primary school. I guess we were best friends, even. But we grew apart once we started going to Balden. She started getting sort of . . . strange.'

Heat swept me as I imagined Abby's face if she could hear this. I hurtled on. 'I mean, she had always been sort of strange, but when we got to secondary school it just got completely sad. She was so out of it; she didn't even *try* to fit in.'

'You mean the way she dressed?' asked Jo. 'Present,' she called to Mrs Conway, who was still struggling away with the register.

I shrugged, playing with a strand of gold-tinted hair, watching it shine in the light. 'Sort of . . . well, we had uniforms, but everyone knew what a Goth she was, with her black fingernails and all. But the worst thing was – she was still, um . . . really into pretend games, like on the playground, and she'd want me to join in.' I forced a laugh. 'Pretty painful.'

'Pretend games?' Jo looked utterly blank. 'Like what?'

'Like, pretending to have magic powers, or that we were in a different world . . .' I trailed off, hearing Karen Stipp's voice. *Look, everyone! Freaky and Geeky are at it again! Ooh, sorry, Freaky, did I break your little magic wand?*

'Weird,' said Debbie, shaking her head.

39

I took a breath. 'Yeah, I know; really weird. So, anyway, we just grew apart, and then in Year Eight I came to school here, and that was the end of it. I hadn't talked to her in ages before I saw her at the bus stop.'

'That's sad.' Jo propped her elbow on the table, leaning her head against her hand. 'I mean, that you used to be such good friends.'

'Yeah, but it happens, doesn't it? People change.' Debbie popped a mint in her mouth and offered the packet to us. 'Anyway, I hope she's OK. Do you think she ran away, or what?'

Oh, *please* can we talk about something else! I looked down, pretending to be searching for the perfect mint. 'Who can say?'

'Well, do you think—'

Jo put her hand on Debbie's arm. 'Stop going on, she doesn't want to talk about it.'

Debbie looked injured. 'I wasn't *going on*. We're her friends! I just asked . . .'

'Friends shut up sometimes,' said Jo firmly.

There was a long pause, with none of us quite knowing where to look. At the front of the room, Mrs Conway had given up on the register, and was reading an announcement about a teachers' meeting the next week. No one was listening to her.

Jo twisted the silver ring on her finger. 'Um – why don't you tell Ems about the contest?'

Debbie smiled in relief. 'Oh, right! It's this fashion design thing; I thought I'd have a go – it's run by *Kiss, Kiss*.' She fumbled in her bag, pulling out the magazine to show me. 'The top ten entries are going

40

to be modelled at a fashion show, with the press there and everything. You both have to help me, OK?'

So of course Jo and I said we would, and we started talking about what sort of outfit Debbie should design, and which of us would model it. 'Why don't we go into town on Saturday?' said Jo. 'Look around the shops, get some ideas.'

And slowly, I felt myself relax. I had got away with it. They still didn't know about Karen.

I rang Mum in Chicago that night, perched on my bed with the cordless phone. When she first moved to America, Dad did loads of shopping around, comparing all the prices (he loves doing that), and he found this really cheap international phone service for me to use, so that I can ring her whenever I want. Mostly we e-mail each other, though. It's like she's turned into my pen-pal or something.

Not that I actually *needed* a pen-pal right now.

'Emma!' she said when she picked up. 'I was just going to ring you . . . are you all right?'

My chest clenched as I twisted the white duvet cover between my fingers. 'No, not really. Mum, something awful's happened—'

'Oh, darling, I know. I just got off the phone with Jenny. I can't believe it. My god; Abby's poor family – I don't know what I'd do if it were you; I'd go mad . . .'

I gripped the phone as she went on, feeling weirdly let down. I guess I wasn't surprised that they had told her, but I still felt a bolt of disappointment that they hadn't left it to me. It was so typical! They were always having secret conferences, the three of them. Four, now that Paul was around. Obviously the world would come to an end if they ever asked *me* what I thought about anything.

'Emma, did you hear me?' Mum's soft voice rose slightly, sounding anxious.

'Sorry, what?'

'I said, do you want me to come home for a while?'

Part of me wanted to shout, *Yes, please!* But how could I tell her to spend thousands of pounds on a plane ticket just to come here and hold my hand?

I plucked at the duvet. 'What about your job?'

Mum works completely stupid hours at the art gallery, like up to twelve hours a day sometimes. When I was in Chicago, I went to a show she'd organized. She says it's hard work to set them up, but during the actual show all she seemed to do was drift about with a glass of champagne, kissing artists on the cheek.

'Don't worry about that; I want to be there for you if you need me. There would be a few things I'd have to tie up, but I could be there in a few days. Maybe a week at the very latest.'

'No, that's OK.' Why didn't she just *come*, instead of making me decide for her!

'Emma, are you sure? I could ring the travel agent this afternoon and sort something; it would be no problem at all.'

'I'm sure,' I said.

There was a pause. I imagined her standing in the gallery, surrounded by weird sculptures and blotches of colour on canvas, twirling a strand of brown hair around her finger. Finally she let out a breath. 'OK, well . . . if you change your mind, give me a ring, all right? I could hop on a plane and be there in less than a day.'

'Yeah, OK.' I hugged myself, staring at the poster of David Beckham on the wall. Becks is gorgeous, that goes without saying, but suddenly I remembered the amazing spaceship poster that I used to have there instead, the one I took down when I started going to St Seb's. I used to love staring at it, imagining travelling to different worlds . . .

'I do hope she's all right,' said Mum in a low voice. Suddenly she sounded like herself again, like she wasn't thousands of miles away any more. 'I remember the two of you toddling around together when you were only three or four years old . . . you were inseparable.'

'Yes, but not *now*!' I blurted out. 'Mum, we weren't even friends any more, not since I changed schools! Why did *I* have to be the last one to see her?'

There was a long pause before Mum answered. 'Darling, I don't know . . . but I do believe that everything happens for a reason.'

Day Four

Hundreds of local volunteers joined in the search for Abby yesterday as the Hampshire Constabulary trawled nearby fields, but nothing was found . . . Abby's parents have appealed to the public for help in finding her, and admit that they fear she has been abducted.

Daily Post, Wednesday 8th September

The video of Abby and her brothers was shown over and over again, hundreds of times. Every time I looked at the TV, there she was, her round face crinkled up with laughter.

'Emma, how long have you known Abby?' asked PC Lavine, sipping at a cup of tea. She and PC Morton had come back to question me again, at home this time.

I had to stop and think. 'Most of my life, I guess. I mean, I used to live across the street from her, and our dads work at the same place.'

'Abby's father and I both work at Clarkson Chemical.' Dad was still wearing his dark grey suit from work. 'She and Abby used to be great friends, but then

45

a couple of years ago Abby started . . . well, going a bit wild, I suppose. So Emma asked if I'd send her to St Sebastian's, which I was more than happy to do. The academic standards are higher, and she's made friends now with some really nice, decent girls—'

Flames scorched up my neck and cheeks. '*Dad,*' I hissed. 'Will you stop? It's not like Abby isn't *decent.*'

Dad looked annoyed as he glanced at me. He hates to be interrupted. 'Well, you were the one who wanted to go to St Sebastian's, love.'

'Yes, but *that's* not why,' I muttered under my breath. But I knew he thought I had been so upset all of Year Seven because of Abby going off the rails or whatever, and that that's why I had wanted to change schools. Well, why wouldn't he think that? It's only what I had *told* him. Because there had been no way that I was going to enlighten him with what had really happened.

I wasn't going to now, either. I looked down, fiddling with my watchband.

PC Morton was watching me keenly. 'Emma, can you tell us how Abby started "going a bit wild", as your dad put it?'

My face scalded. 'She didn't . . . I mean, she's just really into Goth stuff, that's all. She's never done drugs or anything like that.'

'Not so far as you know,' said PC Morton. 'But you haven't been in touch with her for some time, have you?'

'I still know what she's like,' I muttered, looking down. I was *so* aware of Dad sitting there, nodding his head like he had been right all along. He had hardly even seen Abby since she was around seven, which is when he moved out of our house!

PC Lavine put her teacup on the table. Her voice was warm and soothing, like sinking into a hot bath. 'Emma, when you were on the bus with Abby, did you notice any of the other passengers?'

They quizzed me over every aspect of the bus ride again, in mind-numbing detail. If possible, I think it went even worse this time. I really tried, but the whole thing seemed like a dream now, as if the details of the bus ride were a fuzzy nursery rhyme I had learned once. After a while, Jenny started making tea for Nat and the smell of pizza and chips wafted in from the kitchen.

Finally PC Morton nodded, flipping his notebook closed with a sigh. 'Right, Emma, I think that's all for now.'

We all stood up, and PC Lavine touched my shoulder. 'You've been wonderful, Emma. Thanks so much for your help.'

After they left, Dad shook his head. 'My god, poor Ann and Charles. The writing's really on the wall by now, I'm afraid.' Rubbing his forehead, he went to the fish tank and dribbled pellets into the water.

'What do you mean?' Icy fear swept over me. Ann and Charles were Abby's parents.

Dad turned and frowned at me. His voice sounded almost harsh. 'Listen, Emma, I want you to promise me that you'll always be careful, all right? Stick with your friends, don't go off places on your own. The world's full of nutters, unfortunately.'

I felt like I was going to shatter into pieces. I knew what he really meant; I knew what he thought had happened to Abby. Oh, god – it couldn't be true, could it?

'All right, love?' He came over and hugged me. Suddenly I was shaking, and I buried my head in his arm. 'Just be sensible, that's all,' he said, smoothing my hair.

The bottom of my wardrobe was a complete tip, with heaps of old clothes and games shoved into it like a jumble sale. Dressed in the oversized blue T-shirt I wear to bed, I crouched on the floor and started pulling things out – an old scarf, a stuffed walrus called Simpson, a pair of boots.

The box was still there, nestled in the very back of the wardrobe. I sat back on my heels, staring at it. It felt like some ancient archaeological relic. I started to drag it out, and then stopped.

Nothing had changed, really, had it? What was in the box had nothing to do with me any more. The carpet prickled against my bare knees as I crouched there, running my fingers over the cardboard lid.

Isn't that sweet! Freaky is writing a story! Hey, everyone, listen to this – 'The two novice mages . . .' Oi! Quit trying to grab, you rude cow!

My stomach lurched like I had just drunk a pint of rancid milk. I slammed the box back into place and went to bed.

Day Five

We were sitting having breakfast when the phone rang. Jenny started to get it, but Dad stood up, tossing his paper onto the table. He leaned against the kitchen counter. 'Hello?'

'Come on, Natalie, eat up. We're going to be late.' Jenny reached over and started cutting up Nat's sausage for her.

'I *am* eating . . . Mummy, stop it! I can do it myself.'

'What?' said Dad sharply.

I looked up, and saw that his gaze was on me.

'Well, I don't know. When would you be filming?' There was a pause. 'That's awfully short notice . . . well, yes, of course it's an urgent situation, but I have to think what's best for my daughter, as well . . .'

My chair turned to ice, locking me in place. Jenny had gone totally still, watching Dad.

'Let me take your number,' said Dad finally. He scrawled something on the purple post-it pad that Jenny kept by the phone. 'Right . . . I'll discuss it with her and ring you straight back.'

Hanging up the phone, Dad let out a long breath.

He clicked the kettle on. 'Emma . . . the police want you to take part in a filmed re-enactment of Abby's disappearance.'

I licked my lips. 'What would I have to do?'

'Stand at a bus stop with the girl who's playing Abby, sit on a bus with her . . . they're trying to get more witnesses who might have seen Abby to come forward. The only thing is, they're filming this afternoon.' Dad made a cup of instant coffee, frowning down at the bright green mug as he stirred it.

'What show is this for?' asked Jenny.

'*Crimewatch*. They want to air it tomorrow night.'

'You mean – I'd be on TV?' I could actually *feel* all the blood draining from my face.

He nodded. 'If you want to do it. It's up to you, I suppose. The police think it's a good idea, that it might help to find Abby.'

'Then I . . . I have to do it, don't I?'

Jenny squeezed my hand. 'Don't worry, I'll come with you.'

'Right . . .' Dad scraped a hand through his hair. He didn't look overjoyed. 'I'll ring them back, then.'

So I didn't go to school that day. Instead I changed out of my uniform back into the embroidered jeans and sleeveless blue top I had been wearing on Saturday, and Jenny and I drove into Brookfield.

The girl who was playing Abby was about the right height and weight, I guess, but her features were totally different – her face was thin, and she had a snub nose. She was wearing a long black wig, and the standard black Goth outfit. Except that her T-shirt had lots of little grey skulls on it, instead of a screaming green one.

It felt very, very strange to be standing next to her.

The director, Mr Persac, put a hand on my shoulder as he introduced us. 'Emma, this is Sheila Langley; she's a friend of Abby's who's volunteered to help . . . and Sheila, this is Emma Townsend. She used to go to school with Abby, and was the last one to see her.'

Sheila had seemed friendly enough before – we had sort of smiled and nodded at each other – but now she stiffened. 'Oh. Right,' she said coldly.

I swallowed, wondering what her problem was. We stood at the bus stop without talking to each other while people with cameras scurried around, setting things up.

I could see Jenny on the sidelines, talking to Abby's mum. At first glance, I thought she looked more like herself again – her hair was back in its usual soft waves – but then I saw her face, how puffy and vulnerable it looked. She saw me watching her, and gave me a sad smile.

Go say something! Go tell her you're sorry about Abby, and hope she's all right! I couldn't move. Mrs Ryzner probably hated me now. I mean, she wasn't thick; she had to have noticed that I had kept away from their house for a *year.*

Gripping my elbows tightly, I looked away.

The sequence inside the bus took the longest to film. Sheila and I ended up sitting on the same hot, sticky seat together for ages, waiting for them to get the cameras and lights set up. Sheila had an ancient blue rucksack at her feet. When Mr Persac told us, we were supposed to re-enact the bit about the necklace and the book and everything.

The silence between us felt like I was being smothered. Oh, don't be such a drama queen, I told myself. Not everyone is out to get you; haven't you at least figured *that* out, this last year? You probably just imagined her reaction before. Just be friendly. Be *Ems*.

So I tried to smile at her. 'Do you have a copy of the book? *The Monster Manual*, or whatever it is?'

Sheila stopped drumming her (black-painted) fingernails on the windowsill, and gave me this look like I was several degrees thicker than a cretin.

'Yes, I have a copy of *the book*.' Every word dripped with sarcasm, like acid that would splutter and hiss when it hit the ground.

I gripped the bus seat. OK, so I wasn't imagining it. She *loathed* me. 'Um . . . is something wrong?'

Within the black-ringed makeup, Sheila's eyes were very blue, and hard as marbles. 'I'm a friend of Abby's, all right? *You* work it out.'

Guilt curdled through me. I bit my lip, wondering what Abby had told her.

'Right, girls, I think we're about ready to start,' called Mr Persac.

There wasn't a script. Mr Persac had sat us both down beforehand, going over the gist of what Abby and I had said. Sheila and I were supposed to just talk, like we were really Emma and Abby. Most of what we said wouldn't be included in the sequence; the audience would just see me talking to Abby while a voice-over described what had happened.

But there was one bit that Mr Persac did want to be exactly the same as what had happened, and that was Abby's parting shot to me.

'Do we really have to film *that*?' I was ready to dissolve with embarrassment, especially with Sheila's narrowed, smirking eyes watching my every move.

Mr Persac nodded. 'Yes, I'm afraid so. You see, it might be that someone on the bus will remember that she called out after you, and then make the connection that they saw where Abby got off.'

Fine. So Sheila and I acted it out when he told us, with me making comments like, 'How are Greg and Matthew?' et cetera, et cetera. And Sheila clearly adored the bit where she called out, 'You'd really love D&D . . . or at least, the *old* you would have.'

Each time she said it, I felt like jumping off the bus. While it was still moving.

'Right, excellent. Now, just sit tight for a tick, girls,' said Mr Persac. 'We'll go for a final take in a minute.' He was up at the front of the bus, having a word with the driver. The bus had stopped for the moment, but we were actually driving around during the filming, taking the same route that the 56 took.

I sank down beside Sheila again, staring straight ahead. But I could actually *feel* her glaring at me, like little holes were starting to sizzle and smoke in the side of my head. I cleared my throat, trying not to let my voice waver.

'Look – um, I don't know what Abby told you, but—'

Sheila snorted. 'Oh, not much. Just about how you were absolute best friends for years, and then you dumped her for no reason once you went off to St Seb's. About how she kept trying to text you and get together or whatever, but you always fobbed her off with completely lame excuses, and—'

Pressure built up inside me as she spoke, like roaring water held back by a dam. Then the dam shattered, and my words came crashing out. 'Right, so she told you all that! Well, did she tell you about Karen Stipp? Did she mention *anything at all* about Karen Stipp?'

Sheila's face screwed up like she had smelled something putrid. 'Who's *Karen Stipp*?'

My nails dug half-moons into my palms. 'Well, if you don't *know*, then maybe you should just – just—'

'I know enough,' said Sheila icily, and she turned to stare out the window.

A small crowd was waiting when the bus finally pulled back into the station, like we had just returned from an epic voyage. I burst down the steps, scanning the crowd for Jenny's tumble of brown curls. Then she was there, giving me a hug. 'I'm really proud of you, Emma . . . are you all right?'

Yes, except for this psycho girl who hates me. I nodded against her shoulder. 'I guess so.'

She squeezed my arm as we pulled apart. 'You'll be fine,' she said firmly.

We both looked up as Mr Persac came over. His face was like Dad's after a long day – tired and drained, but still trying to smile. 'Emma, thanks for your help today. You did a splendid job, really first-rate.'

'I just hope it helps find her,' said Jenny softly.

Mr Persac sighed. 'Well, we'll see. The show does tend to get a good response; it's just whether any of it will turn out to be useful or not.'

'How does it work?' asked Jenny. 'Will you show it more than once?'

I heard Sheila's voice behind me, and turned. She was standing a couple of meters away, talking with Abby's mum. As I watched, Sheila gave Mrs Ryzner a hug, and they clung to each other like they were drowning. A slight blond woman – Sheila's mother, I guessed – stood to one side.

A golf ball formed in my throat. Inanely, I noticed that Sheila had taken off the black wig. Her own hair was short and blond, teased up in spikes. She must have used an eyebrow pencil to darken her eyebrows.

Jenny turned. 'Are you ready to go, love?'

I nodded quickly, tearing my gaze away. We had to walk right past them to get back to our car, though, and Jenny stopped, stepping into the little group and touching Mrs Ryzner's arm. 'Ann, please, let us know if there's anything at all we can do . . .'

'Yes, I will . . . and Emma, thank you so much for your help.'

Her round face – so much like Abby's – was totally

sincere; she was actually *grateful* to me. I wanted to hug her so badly, but I couldn't. I felt about two centimetres high. Thanks for dumping my daughter. Thanks for being horrible to her on the bus.

Sheila was openly glaring at me, not even pretending to be civil. 'That's OK,' I managed finally.

As we left, I heard Sheila say, 'When should we come around for the posters?'

'Tonight's fine. Sheila, you and the others have just been wonderful . . .' Then Jenny and I rounded the corner of the bus station, and I couldn't hear any more.

But I had heard the warmth in Mrs Ryzner's voice, and it felt like a cold, clammy towel had been thrown over me. She used to be like a second mum to me. She had called Abby and me her two girls.

I stared down at my feet as we walked the short distance to the car park, and thought about how Abby must have felt when I didn't return her texts. When I always had to get off the phone about two seconds after she rang. I had totally hardened myself to it at the time, but she must have been gutted.

We got to the car, and Jenny stood rummaging in her handbag for her keys, muttering, 'Oh, come on . . . they were here just a second ago.' I leaned against the warm metal, trying not to cry.

OK, it was an awful thing to do, but I had had enough of being a *freak,* that was all! After everything that happened, I would have been mad to stay friends with Abby. I wasn't a terrible person!

Really? asked a little voice in my head.

Day Six

I was at Debbie's house with Jo when the *Crimewatch* episode aired. We had decided to look through some magazines, to get ideas for the fashion contest before we went shopping the next day. Or at least that's what Debbie had said. But the moment all of us were sprawled across the carpet with copies of *Vogue* and *Now,* Jo said, 'So, um – how are you doing, Ems?'

From the way Debbie looked up quickly from her *Vogue,* I knew that they had planned this, the two of them. My chest clenched as I tried to laugh, flipping through a magazine.

'I'm totally fine. Come on, you know that – you just saw me at school today.'

Jo shifted, drawing her legs up under her. 'Yeah, but – I mean, you seem—'

'I'm fine. Oh, Debbie, look, here's the sort of dress you want.' I slid the magazine across the carpet towards her. 'You'd look just *sizzlingly* sexy. I mean, seriously, steam would be coming off you.'

For a second Debbie looked like she was going to say something else, and then she smiled slightly.

'Well . . . that goes without saying. I'm just a super-model, me.'

I could feel Jo's eyes on me. Finally she smiled, too. 'Hang on, I thought *I* was modelling it.'

'Nah, you're too tall,' said Debbie. 'And leggy and blond. No way are you model-material.'

'Oh, sorry – didn't realize *short* was a requirement.'

'She'll be the most gorgeous munchkin at the ball,' I said. 'Look at this one, Debbie – what do you think?'

We kept the banter going, leafing through the magazines and laughing, but it almost felt like we were reading lines. Not to mention that Jo and Debbie kept darting these concerned looks at each other when they thought I couldn't see.

Part of me ached to talk to them, to tell them all about Abby, and how scared I felt, but I couldn't. What if I slipped up, and mentioned Karen? What if they found out how pathetic I had been – Emma, the cringing joke of Balden? I clutched the slick page of *Now,* staring down at the model. No way. I was never going to be that person again.

Then the programme came on.

'Should I change the channel?' Debbie's green eyes cut towards me doubtfully.

'No, that's OK.'

Jo straightened up. 'Ems, are you sure?'

Ems was completely sure. 'Yeah, I'm fine. Just leave it on.' I turned a glossy page, pretending to be engrossed in an article on plastic surgery.

'Tonight our focus is on missing Hampshire teenager, Abby Ryzner. Abby went shopping in Brookfield last Saturday, took the bus home – and hasn't been seen for six days, despite increasingly desperate pleas from her family, and a police hunt that has involved over a hundred officers . . .'

My eyes kept drifting towards the screen. Finally I gave up pretending, and shoved the magazine away.

Sheila hadn't looked at all like Abby in real life, but now I could hardly tell the difference. We watched her say goodbye to Mrs Ryzner, walk around the shops in town – and it was even Abby's *expression;* that sort of dreamy, not-quite-there look.

Then I came on, and it was just bizarre, like someone had been hiding behind the next seat over, filming Abby and me. I watched us talking on the bus, with the familiar streets and buildings trundling past the window, and goose pimples scattered across my arms. It was like watching a pair of ghosts. *Turn it off!* I wanted to scream, but the words wouldn't come.

When Sheila called out her infamous line, I winced despite myself. Jo touched my arm. 'Are you OK?'

'Sure,' I said, not looking at her. On the screen, a number was flashing for people to ring if they had seen Abby.

Finally, finally, the segment ended. Debbie sat up, pushing her dark hair out of her eyes. 'Um . . . so what's D&D, anyway?'

Jo sat up too, the same question on her face. Like I was some sort of expert, just because Abby had asked me to play. It wasn't as if I had gone *with* her that afternoon.

If I had, would she be missing now? No, don't think about that.

I lifted a shoulder. 'Some sort of game she was into. I don't really know, to be honest . . . it sounded pretty weird when she described it.'

Remember Esmerelda? Sort of like that, but better . . .

Abby's back garden flashed into my mind, heavy with the scent of summer. We were sitting hunched in her playhouse – only it wasn't her playhouse; it was a dungeon in Esmerelda's castle, and the faint sunlight was light through a tiny barred window.

We'll have to try the spell, my friend – we've no choice.

No! It could destroy us both!

And it could save us, too . . .

A wave of longing smashed against me. Abby, please be all right . . .

'Well, how did—' started Debbie.

'It was so stupid!' I burst out. 'She was always doing stuff like that – I mean, she just didn't get it, she just didn't *get* that you don't do that once you get to secondary school!'

Jo and Debbie were staring at me, their eyes like the button-eyes on teddy bears.

'If you want to know the truth, I really couldn't stand her any more.' I grabbed one of the magazines and started flipping through it, slapping the pages back. 'She's why I changed schools, even – she had got so *weird* that I couldn't stick being around her!'

Jo licked her lips, glancing at Debbie. 'Um . . . well, how was she weird?'

'Well, she dressed pretty strangely,' murmured Debbie. Jo flashed her a look.

'Oh, she just *was*, that's all.' I shoved *Now* aside and grabbed at a *Vogue*. 'She acted however she wanted, even if it was completely childish and stupid; she didn't care what people thought – she left herself right open for everything—'

'For what?' Jo's blond eyebrows pulled together in bewilderment.

I swallowed hard. Emma, *shut up*!

'Nothing,' I stared down at a photo of a pencil-thin model wearing a white tube dress. 'Debbie, couldn't you do something like this?' I forced a laugh. 'Looks like it'd be a breeze to design – just wrap a bedsheet around yourself, *et voilà*!'

They looked at each other. Suddenly I was terrified that they wouldn't let me drop it this time, that they'd push and question until it all came out.

But they took the hint. They didn't mention Abby again.

Day Seven

Even though I woke up early that morning, I lay in bed for ages, staring at my ceiling. Thinking of the ceiling of my old room. Abby and I had painted a moonscape on it, with craters and stars, and a view of Earth in the distance. I remembered the two of us standing on ladders with old sheets draped over everything, collapsing in giggles as she painted a bug-eyed purple moon-man, peering out of a crater . . .

'Emma?' came a voice outside my door. Nat, lurking.

'What?' I flopped over in bed, clutching the duvet around me.

Nat poked her head in. Her brown hair looked wild and bedraggled, like she had been playing hard for hours already. 'You're not up yet.'

'Well spotted.'

She slid into the room, shutting the door behind her. She was wearing jeans and a hot pink top with *Ballerina* on it. 'Mummy said to let you sleep. She said you're having a rough time.'

The pillow muffled my voice. 'So why are you in here, not letting me sleep?'

'Because it's Saturday! You said you'd play with me today.'

I was completely positive that I hadn't said anything of the sort, actually. I lay there for a few seconds, thinking about telling her to bugger off, and then I slowly sat up, collapsing the warm cave of covers.

'OK. Come sit here, and we'll play.'

Her face split in delight, and she bounded across the room, bouncing onto the bed. I shoved my hair back. It felt ropy. 'Right . . . where were we?'

'We were entering the chamber where Jasmine awaited!' breathed Nat, her eyes gleaming. 'Wands at the ready!'

That's right. God, that was ages ago. 'OK, close your eyes.'

She popped them closed, leaning against me. I put my arm around her sturdy little body, feeling her warmth, and lowered my voice to a whisper. 'Now, Jasmine's chamber is made of . . . of seashells. The insides of seashells, all sort of shimmering pink and grey. Can you see them yet?'

Nat's hair tickled my arm as she shook her head, eyes still closed.

'Keep trying. Seashells, glistening on the walls . . . Just think about Jasmine's palace, and you'll be there.'

'Ooh, I can see it!' she breathed. 'And Jasmine's sitting on a throne of shells! She looks *evil*!'

'She is, but we have to go in and face her. She has green hair, like seaweed, and as we approach her, she sort of draws herself up and says—'

Both of us started as someone knocked on my door.

'What?' I called.

'Phone's for you,' said Jenny. 'Someone called Sheila.' She opened the door and tossed me the cordless extension, rolling her eyes as she spotted her wayward daughter. 'I told you not to come in here, didn't I? Come on now, let Emma take her call in peace.'

'No! We're playing a game . . . !'

'We'll finish later, Nat.' I stared down at the extension like it was about to explode in my face. *Sheila?*

Nat flung herself dramatically off the bed, and Jenny drew her out of the room. As the door shut behind them, I took a deep breath and picked up the phone. 'Um . . . hello?'

'Emma, it's Sheila. From the re-enactment.' Her voice sounded as spiky as her hair.

'Yeah, I know.'

'Look, I'm ringing because a group of us got together last night to watch *Crimewatch*. A group of Abby's *friends,* I mean. And since we're closer to her than anyone, right, we're going to try to figure out what's happened to her. And we have some questions we'd like to ask you.'

'But the police have already—'

'*Duh,* yes, obviously. They've spoken to all of us, too, but we want to have a go ourselves. So we're meeting at my house this morning . . . if it's not too much trouble for you to come around, that is.'

What, go to her *house?* How could I face Abby's friends when they all hated me? I licked dry lips. 'Um – how did you get my number, anyway?'

She huffed out a breath. 'There are fourteen

Townsends in the phonebook. *T* Townsend, presumably your father, is number twelve. Look, I don't have time for this – we're all going to be here at eleven o'clock, and it's number four Auburn Street in Garemont. If you want to help Abby, you'll turn up . . . though I really don't expect you will.'

Click.

Of course I wasn't going. I'd have to be completely barking! It would be suicidal to go present myself to a bunch of Abby's friends – like sauntering into the lions' den, only worse. At least the lions don't have anything against you personally as they rip you to shreds.

I got out of bed, throwing the covers back. I was due to meet Debbie and Jo at one o'clock, in the town centre, and it was only around half nine now – I'd have a nice, relaxing morning, maybe go for a swim with Jenny.

I paused in front of my wardrobe, staring at my clothes. Yeah, a relaxing morning . . . except that I kept hearing Sheila's voice buzzing in my ears, taunting me. *If you want to help Abby . . .*

They hated me, though. They *hated* me. My stomach lurched as I pulled on a pair of jeans. When I glanced in the mirror, my expression stared back at me, wide-eyed.

Abby would do it for me, even if we hadn't spoken for *ten* years, let alone one.

Slowly, I finished getting dressed. My fingers were cold and clumsy, and when I looked at myself in the mirror again, I didn't exactly look determined.

Turning away from the sight of my pale face, I snatched up my handbag and left, shutting the door behind me.

I told Dad and Jenny I was going into town, and then took the bus to Sheila's house. It was the number 56, the same one I had taken with Abby, exactly a week ago now. Hopefully it wasn't the same exact bus. Trying not to think about it, I stared out at the familiar shops and houses, wondering if I had gone completely mental. *Why* was I doing this?

Auburn Street was just a minute or so away from where I used to live. I stood on the doorstep of number four for ages, watching my finger hover over the doorbell. Finally I clenched my jaw and jabbed it hard. Crossing my arms over my chest, I listened to the sound of approaching footsteps, willing myself not to run.

The door flew open and it was Sheila standing there, wearing a black T-shirt with a dragon on it, and about twenty silver earrings. Her eyes widened when she saw me. Then she tossed her head and the familiar sneer dropped back into place.

'Oh, so you actually came. Well, come on then – we're all upstairs in my room.'

She shut the door behind me and stalked up the stairs, her back ramrod-straight. I swallowed and followed her, neither of us saying a word.

I don't know what I expected – black and more black, I suppose – but Sheila's room had these amazing fantasy posters everywhere, and a prism hanging in front of the window that scattered tiny rainbow-lights across the room.

'That's Rob, and that's Gail,' said Sheila, flopping onto the bed. 'This is *Emma*, everyone.'

Rob gave me a sort of salute – a gangly, dark-haired boy in a flapping black trenchcoat. Gail was heavy-set with crimson hair, wearing a black corset-type dress with dramatically flowing sleeves. She nodded at me. 'Hi.'

'Hi.' I hugged my elbow, feeling stupidly trendy in my flared jeans and tight brown top. I sank down on the floor beside Sheila's desk.

Suddenly I saw that there were four cardboard boxes stacked against the wall. Every one of them had a black and white poster of Abby taped to the front. **MISSING: ABIGAIL RYZNER, known as 'Abby'**. I looked quickly away.

'Should we wait for—?' started Rob.

Sheila's earrings rattled as she shook her head. 'No, he said he might be late. Let's just get started.'

Gail drew a notebook out of her bag, opening it to a page with lots of writing. She cleared her throat, not looking at me. 'Um – right, Emma. What did Abby say when she first saw you?'

For a second my brain felt completely out of step. I took a breath. 'Um – well, you know, we said hello . . . it wasn't anything important.'

Sheila rolled her eyes. 'You can't *know* it wasn't important. Come on, what exactly did you say?'

So I struggled to recall exactly what we had said, and Gail scribbled down all the banal stuff about *how's your mum, how are your brothers.* It had been such a nothing conversation, so why did I feel like they were taking my clothes off?

'What did you talk about on the bus?' asked Rob. He had a scattering of acne, and dark eyes that squinted at me like I was a theorem he was trying to work out.

I looked down, picking at a bit of carpet fluff. 'Um . . . she said that she was getting ready to start GM-ing, or whatever it's called, and that her game was going to be more exciting or something . . . she showed me this book, the *Monster Manual* . . .' Gail wrote it all down without commenting, the black lace of her sleeves making a spider-web pattern against her arm.

Against my will, my eyes were drawn to the four boxes again. Feeling sick, I jerked my gaze away, looking instead at the D&D books bulging in Sheila's bookshelf. She had the *Monster Manual,* too.

Sheila's eyes were narrow blue slits, sneering at every word I said. 'What was in her knapsack?' she barked.

I felt my face redden as I glanced at her. 'You already know that from the re-enactment—'

'Remind us, will you?'

'Fine!' My voice wavered. 'There was the box with the necklace in it, and the book – and I think a bottle of Pepsi—'

Her nose jabbed at me like a pointing finger. 'You *think*? Can't you even *try* to remember?'

'I *am*—'

'Look, let's go on to something else,' broke in Rob,

tapping his fingers on the thigh of his jeans. 'What sort of mood was Abby in? Did she seem upset or anything?'

Sheila flopped back against the headboard with her arms across her chest. 'Probably she was fine until Emma here told her to piss off. Right, Emma?'

A prickling burned my throat. 'We were *both* upset; it wasn't like—'

Gail looked up from her notebook. 'Yeah, but do you think the stuff with you was all that was upsetting her? Or was there something else?'

I looked away, trying not to think of the cautiously happy look on Abby's face when she first caught sight of me. I could feel them all watching me. 'It was just – the stuff with me, I guess,' I managed finally.

Sheila's mouth twisted. 'Yeah, what a total surprise. Right, next question. Did you—'

'Look, forget it! This is – I mean, maybe I should just go.' I started to scramble up, grabbing blindly at my handbag.

'No, wait!' Gail held her hand up. 'Come on, Sheila, leave off, will you? She's trying to help us, at least.'

Sheila snorted and looked away.

'OK?' said Gail to me.

My heart thudded as I sank slowly back down again. 'Yeah, whatever. But, um – I have to leave soon.' Coward! Why didn't I just leave *now*?

Rob let out an impatient breath. 'Look, let's get back to Abby. The way I see it, one of three things could have happened to her.'

'Go on, then.' Gail's pen was poised over the notepad.

Rob ticked the options off on his fingers. 'Right. One, she ran away. Two, she had some sort of accident somewhere. Or, three – she was, um, kidnapped.'

'Well, I don't think she ran away,' burst out Sheila.

Gail and Rob stared at her.

'Because . . . she had plans and everything.' Sheila's mouth trembled slightly, and a ferocious scowl darkened her face. 'And frankly, I don't think what happened with *Emma* was enough to make her freak out and run off somewhere.'

That word again, *freak.* As if on cue, all three of them turned and stared at me. Some tiny part of me managed to hold myself together, and I jerked my chin up, staring back at them.

Gail looked away first. Her voice was husky as she spoke. 'And – and if she had an accident between the bus and her house, someone would have found her, wouldn't they? It's only a few minutes away, and it's not like it's – wilderness or anything.'

Silence choked over the room. I pressed against the desk, hugging my knees, and suddenly wanted to say something, *anything*, that would help. But I couldn't. I knew the fear that was gripping all of them, because it was my fear, too – that Abby had been shoved into a car by some psycho murderer, that she had been hurt, terrified . . .

Killed.

Suddenly Sheila swung her feet off the bed. 'What's the point of this, eh? What's the *point* – come on, let's get out of here.'

Rob swallowed. 'But I thought we were—'

'Forget it! It's stupid!' Sheila lunged across the room to the cardboard boxes, hefting one at Rob. 'And *you*—' she spun on me, almost crying. 'Yeah, why don't you just leave . . . we're all Abby's friends here.'

So I did; I left the room, and stumbled down the stairs in a haze. As I got to the bottom, the doorbell rang, and a moment later Sheila and the others came pounding down the stairs, carrying the cardboard boxes.

Sheila shouldered past me and wrenched open the door. A boy with longish blond hair and a pierced eyebrow stood there. 'Thank *god* you're here,' said Sheila. 'Here, take this.'

She shoved one of the boxes at him. He clutched it, glancing at me with a startled frown. 'Um, weren't we going to—'

'Forget it!' snapped Sheila. 'What do you want to talk to *her* for; she's useless, bloody useless—' Without missing a beat, she turned and bellowed, '*Mum! We're leaving!*'

I left, pushing past the boy with the pierced eyebrow. I wasn't about to do the social polite thing with Mrs Langley, when her daughter would happily nail me to a tree.

As I waited for the bus, hugging myself, I saw the four of them fanning out down the street, taping posters to utility poles, walls, sides of houses. Once they had disappeared down the next road, I went over and looked at one. I couldn't stop myself.

Abby Ryzner, 13, missing since Saturday, 4th September . . . She was wearing black trousers, a black T-shirt, and silver jewellery . . . If you have seen Abby, or have any information . . .

Her smiling face looked out at me from inside a plastic folder. I touched it, thinking, I guess they put the posters in plastic to stop them getting wet or whatever . . . oh, very clever, Emma, go to the head of the class! I shoved my hands in my pockets, struggling against tears, and turned and left, heading back to the bus stop.

Or that was my plan. Instead, I found myself walking straight past it and down the next road.

I walked down my old street slowly, feeling like I had just landed from another galaxy. It was all exactly the same, and completely different. The big magnolia tree at the bottom had been cut down. Number twelve had paved their front garden to make a parking space.

Abby's house stood across the street from my old house, a few numbers down, a brick mid-terrace just like all the others. Seeing it again felt like slipping into a favourite old jumper. Abby and I used to practically live in each other's houses, running back and forth across the street a dozen times a day.

Plus we had loads of special places, dotted around the area like pirate treasure. We even made a map of them once – like the cluster of birch trees in the park two streets over, which we decided was a portal to other worlds, and the fence outside a crumbling old house down the road. We'd peer in and make up stories about it . . .

'Emma?' called a man's voice.

I whirled around. Our old next-door neighbour

was standing outside his house, looking quizzically at me.

'Hi, Mr Yates.' I straightened my shoulders, trying to look casual. Right, like I just *happened* to be strolling past.

Mr Yates came over and leaned against the gate, his bald head gleaming in the sun. 'Aye, I thought that was you. How's your mum doing? Enjoying America?'

So there was a bit of small talk – yes, she's fine, she loves it – and all the while I was dreading the conversation turning to Abby, inevitably, like an earthquake. Sure enough, finally he said, 'Come to help the Ryzners with their posters, have you?'

I glanced over at their house again. It looked so weirdly silent, like a relic from a ghost town. I shrugged, swallowing hard. 'Yeah . . . I thought I could help.'

'Good for you! I've put some up myself, but it's a bit hard to fit in with work. Still, you want to do whatever you can, don't you?' Mr Yates shook his head. 'Such a terrible thing . . . well, Charles is in now, I think, if you want to pop across.'

He turned away, dead-heading pink and purple flowers from the hanging basket beside his door. I just stood there, gulping like a fish. *How* had I got into this?

He glanced back at me, eyebrows up. 'Go on, pet; he's in.'

No, I can't, I have to leave now. I made a mistake; I didn't mean it! I couldn't say any of it, not with Mr Yates staring at me.

'Yes, OK. Thanks.' And before I could think about it, I turned and crossed the street.

The closer I got to Abby's house, the spookier it seemed. It was just . . . silent. I could practically hear the forsythia bush rustling in the wind.

The Ryzner's house used to be anything but silent. You could hardly approach it without being deafened by the wall of sound that was Abby's music, or being flattened by Greg and Matthew as they came roaring out of the house.

The Terrible Twins. We used to have mini-wars with them, plotting these elaborate campaigns in Abby's playhouse. *Ten Things to do to the TTs.* Boiling oil, we decided, and cascaded dead leaves and twigs over them the next time they tried to invade.

Feeling Mr Yates' eyes still on me, I took a deep breath and rang the bell.

'And this was taken last summer . . . I think you had moved away by then, hadn't you?' Mr Ryzner rubbed his stubble-laden chin as he stared at a photo of Abby on a beach. His throat moved, and he passed it to me quickly, diving back into the stack of photos in front of him.

'This is on the Costa again . . . she and Greg got very into building sand castles . . .'

'Wow, that's really artistic,' I said weakly.

I was sitting, trapped at the Ryzner's massive dining table as photo after photo of Abby piled up beside me. When I had asked whether they needed any help putting up posters, Mr Ryzner had started out talking very matter-of-factly about how many posters they had, and how they had decided which photo to use, and then somehow this had drifted into him bringing out their holiday snaps. And now he looked like he was about to cry.

'This was a nice one . . . we almost used this one, actually, except she wasn't . . . wasn't wearing the sort of clothes she usually wears . . .'

I nodded, clutching a mug of almost-cold tea that I hadn't wanted and couldn't drink. In the kitchen, I could hear Abby's grandmother moving about, talking softly to herself in Polish. I longed to be in there with her, smiling and nodding and not understanding a word she said.

Mrs Ryzner and the twins were out putting up posters. 'I'd be helping them, but someone has to be here to catch the phone, you see . . . if it rings . . .' Mr Ryzner had tried to smile when he said this. It was horrible.

'And this is one of Abby and her mum . . . it's amazing; she's as tall as Ann now, isn't she . . .'

Suddenly I knew that I would disintegrate if I sat there another moment. I jumped up, scraping my chair back. 'Um, Mr Ryzner – I'll be right back, I have to go to the loo.'

He nodded, frowning down at the photo like it held the answer to a cosmic puzzle.

After I used the upstairs toilet, I washed my hands in cold water, staring at myself in the mirror. My eyes looked hunted. I didn't want to go downstairs again, not for anything. But I couldn't stay up here, could I?

I glanced longingly at the window. There was a tree outside . . . Oh, right! Ems makes her great escape, scampering nimbly, squirrel-like, to the ground. I sighed and dried my hands on a soft red towel. No. *Ems* wouldn't even be here. It was just me, Emma, completely awkward as always.

Finally I couldn't put it off any longer. I opened the door and stepped back into the familiar corridor. Family pictures of Ryzners stretching back four generations covered the walls like a patchwork quilt.

Abby's room was the second on the right.

I didn't mean to go into it. It was the last thing I wanted to do, actually. But it drew me like a magnet. I walked the few steps to her room, and put my hand on the doorknob.

I paused, glancing down the corridor towards the stairs. And then I eased open the door.

The familiar riot of colour jumped out at me. It looked just the same. I slipped into the room and closed the door, plunging back in time as I took in the overflowing bookshelves, the walls covered with fantasy images.

If you added up all the time I had spent in here, I bet it would be months. Years.

She had a *Lord of the Rings* poster; that was new. I looked at the gorgeous guy who played Legolas, with his liquid dark eyes, and remembered how entranced I had been by the first film when I saw it last year. Or would have been, if I hadn't been so worried about Jo and Debbie loathing every second. They were actually *laughing* in parts of it. Gingerly, I sat on the bed, staring around me. I used to sleep over here practically every other weekend. We'd sit up and talk until three in the morning. I saw Abby lying in bed with her arms crossed under her head, her thick dark hair fanned out across the pillow.

Imagine you could build your own private world – what would it be like?

Um, let me think. It would be a water world, with lots of tropical islands, as far as the eye can see . . . turquoise blue water shimmering everywhere.

And warm, right? It has to be warm!

Oh yeah, blazing sun. And you'd ride to other islands on sort of like unicorns, but they'd swim . . .

What, like mer-unicorns?

Yeah, why not? Mericorns.

Sounds great. Plunging through the water . . .

Galloping over the waves . . . And there'd be palaces rising up out of the water, too, built of – you know, that glisteny stuff inside of shells . . .

Emma, you should write a story about this! It sounds fantastic, really great . . .

I swiped angrily at my eyes and jumped from the bed, ready to dash downstairs and throw some excuse at Mr Ryzner, *any* excuse as to why I had to go home, right now. But then my gaze caught on Abby's dresser. In the middle of a display of photos of family and friends, there was a photo of the two of us, in a carved wooden frame.

I walked over and picked it up.

The photo looked lushly leafy and green, with Abby and I both barefoot, smiling into the camera with our arms around each other's shoulders. I remembered that day – it was when Mum had taken us to the New Forest when we were eight.

It was all so simple then.

As I put the photo back, it bumped against a silver dragon figurine, knocking it over with a tiny clatter. I started to straighten it – and instead my hand closed around it, and I picked it up. Small, but heavier than it looked. It sat coiled in my palm, its wings flared open.

A door banged shut downstairs, and my heart went berserk. I leapt for the corridor, closing the door behind me.

Downstairs, Abby's father was still just sitting at the dining table, staring at photos. The door to the lounge had been shut; the sound of a TV drifted out.

Abby's gran. My shoulders sagged with relief; I had thought that Mrs Ryzner and the twins might have come home. And if *Sheila* hated me, I could imagine how Greg and Matthew felt.

'Well, um . . . I should probably go now, Mr Ryzner.' My smile felt pasted onto my lips. 'But if you have any spare posters that you'd like me to put up, just let me know, OK . . . ?'

The hair lifted on my arms as Mr Ryzner glanced at me with a confused frown, like he didn't know who I was for a second. Then his face cleared and he stood up, clearing his throat. Suddenly he was Mr Efficient, all bustle and purpose.

'Posters, yes, of course. Just wait a second, I'll get you a box.'

As he went into the other room, I realized that I

was still clutching the little dragon. I knew that I should turn around and put it straight back in Abby's room. Or at least chuck it on the piano or something, for someone to find later.

But instead, I tucked it in my jeans pocket.

As I rode the bus home, the posters sat perched on the seat beside me like a mute passenger. I stared at them, feeling like my stomach had been tied into one of those complex sailor's knots. Apart from everything else, I was supposed to be in Brookfield in about twenty minutes, to meet Jo and Debbie at the shops!

The bus trundled slowly up Salt Hill. I had purposely placed the box so that I couldn't see Abby's photo on the poster taped to the front, but now I nudged it around, looking at her round-cheeked face.

I wanted to help, I really did. But how was I supposed to put up posters? What if someone from Balden saw me doing it? *What's wrong, Emma? Lost your freaky friend? Ooh, I hope that nasty Esmerelda hasn't magicked her away!*

I slumped down in my seat, hating myself for being so craven.

Finally I sent a text to Jo, saying I'd be late, and then got off the bus at my stop, dragging the heavy box the ten-minute walk to my house. I had sweat stains under my arms when I got there. But at least Jenny and Dad were out in the garden, so I was spared the interrogation. I could see them through the back door, along with Nat, who was dancing around in her bathing suit with a hose.

I took the box upstairs and shoved it under my bed.

I didn't know what to do with the dragon. I held it in my hand for a long time, feeling its weight. Finally I hid it in the drawer of my bedside table, shutting it away with pens and an old journal. And then felt a pang of sadness, like he might get lonely in there, all by himself.

I shook my head, blowing my breath out in an irritated puff. Get a grip!

I changed my shirt and left to go meet Jo and Debbie.

'What do you think of this?' Debbie leaned her sketch-book towards us. The three of us were sitting in Café Nero later that afternoon, drinking cappuccinos. Or fiddling with them, in my case.

'Excellent! That's a complete award-winner!' Jo sat propped forward in the silver café chair, inspecting Debbie's drawing. She had decided on a sort of harem theme, with hip-hugging swirly trousers and a scanty top.

'Completely brilliant, Debs. I love the, um – purple bits.' I looked down, stirring the chocolate into my coffee.

There was a pause, and then Jo let out a breath. 'Look, Ems, enough of this, OK? You're obviously really upset about Abby, and we don't think you should . . . pretend everything's OK.'

Debbie nodded, snapping her sketchbook closed. 'We're worried about you,' she said flatly. 'We think you need to talk about it more. We're your friends; we want to help.'

Warmth radiated through me, and suddenly I was ridiculously close to tears. Maybe I could talk to them, really *talk* to them, and it would be OK. Maybe I could even tell them – everything.

'Thanks, you two.' I drew my sleeve across my face, and Jo dived into her handbag to hand me a tissue.

'OK?' she asked gently.

I nodded, dabbing at my leaking eyes. 'Um, it's just been so – I mean, I'm worried about her all the time, and – I keep imagining all the things that might have happened to her, or *be* happening to her . . .'

Jo and Debbie sat very still, nodding as I spoke. Behind us, I could hear someone ordering a café latte. I looked down, clicking my spoon against my saucer. 'But the worst thing is – well, the way I, um . . . treated her, after I left Balden. See, we—'

'Emma?' As Jo and Debbie's gazes flicked behind me, I turned around in my seat – and almost passed out, right across the table and our cappuccinos.

Karen Stipp was standing there.

She looked just the same – tall and confident, with wavy golden-brown hair and dark eyes. And dressed perfectly as usual, in tight black trousers and a shiny white top.

She smiled at me, just like she hadn't completely ruined my life at Balden. 'Emma, hi . . . I haven't seen you in ages.'

No, what a surprise! I tend to avoid people who make my life an utter misery.

'Oh . . . hi, Karen.' Suddenly I felt like a neon sign was blazing on my forehead: pathetic Emma, the freak of Balden. I bit my lip and glanced at Jo and Debbie, who were looking at Karen with interest. Somehow I managed to introduce everybody.

Karen scraped a chair over to our table, sitting down uninvited with her coffee. 'Emma, listen, are you OK? We're all really worried about Abby at Balden, so I can imagine how *you* must feel.'

She actually sounded concerned. I gripped my coffee cup warily. 'Um – yeah, I'm OK.'

Karen glanced at Jo and Debbie. 'Emma and Abby used to be really close. It's so awful, not knowing if she's OK or not. I have Abby for a few classes at school, and now it's like there's this gaping space where she sat . . .'

I took a slurp of coffee as emotions crashed inside me like tidal waves. This could not be true – Karen Stipp being nice!

Jo nodded. 'We were just talking about Abby . . . it's really scary.'

'Yeah, it is.' Karen took a pack of chocolates from her handbag and offered us all one. Her eyes were wide and innocent as she looked at me. 'Emma, doesn't it just seem really *freaky* to you? The way it's all happened?'

I froze in my seat, splinters of terror icing through me. A tiny, questioning smile hovered on Karen's face. Oh, god – any moment now, she'd tell Jo and Debbie what had happened at Balden; she'd *tell* them.

'Um – yeah.' I strangled the words out. 'It just . . . yeah.'

'It's sort of hard for her to talk about,' said Debbie, unwrapping a chocolate.

'Oh, of course.' Karen stirred her coffee, looking down like she was embarrassed to have even brought it up. She glanced over at Debbie's sketchbook, which had some drawings on the front cover. 'Hey, whose is this? These are really good.'

Before I knew it, Debbie was showing Karen her drawings for the fashion contest, and Karen was gushing all over them, saying things like, 'Wow, that's *fantastic* – but have you thought about making this bit in gold? I think gold would go *so-o* well with the turquoise.'

And Jo and Debbie were smiling, chatting away to her, with Debbie scribbling down Karen's ideas like they were precious coins of wisdom. When they weren't looking, Karen smirked at me over her coffee. *Freak,* she mouthed.

My stomach lurched as I clutched my cappuccino. Oh my god, how could this be *happening*? Why couldn't she just leave me alone! And now Jo and Debbie liked Karen; they *liked* her. They had forgotten all about me, they were too busy matey-ing it up with a girl who despised me to even notice how upset I was!

Finally Jo glanced over at me, and had the grace to look guilty. 'Oh, Ems, I'm sorry! You were talking about Abby.'

'No, that's OK. I don't really feel like talking about it, anyway.' I rotated my coffee cup on the saucer, carefully aligning the handle at a perfect angle. Karen was sitting back in her seat smiling sadly at me, like she *so* understood what I was going through.

Debbie shut her sketchbook, shoving it down into

her bag. 'Listen Ems, I've got a great idea . . . why don't you and Jo come around to my house Monday night? Kirsten is coming over for tea, and we could all sit around and work on my designs. You know, sort of get your mind off things.' Kirsten is her older sister, who's studying art at Southampton University.

'Well – yeah, OK. Sounds good.' The knots in my stomach relaxed enough for me to smile at her, and she and Jo looked really pleased. Bollocks to Karen. These were my friends; she couldn't ruin it for me.

But then Debbie said to Karen, 'Hey, you could come too, if you like. You had some great ideas.'

I probably looked like I had swallowed a flapping great moth. No one noticed; Jo and Debbie were too busy smiling at their new best buddy. She grinned back at them, brushing a strand of her honey-coloured hair off her face. 'Oh, I'd really like to, but we're having a birthday party for my gran on Monday night. Some other time, OK?'

And the next thing I knew, the three of them were exchanging mobile numbers.

When I got home I escaped upstairs, scooping Pippin up from his favourite perch on the landing and shutting myself in my room. I popped a CD in and curled up tightly on my bed. Pippin cuddled beside me, purring, and I stroked him, trying not to cry.

I hated Karen. I hated her. It wasn't enough that she had made my life hell at Balden; she had to ruin things for me now, too! And Jo and Debbie—

I blinked back tears as my gaze lingered on Darth

Vader in his menacing pose, black cape swirling. And I remembered the first time Jo and Debbie came around to my house last year, and how they had thought Darth was just a scream. Like, that I was being *post-ironic* or something, having a Darth Vader alarm clock.

So of course I had to go along with it. Flip my hair back and drawl, 'Yeah, pretty sad, isn't it? *Use the force* . . . It makes me cringe so much every morning that I get up just to avoid it.'

I wiped my face on Pippin's fur, sniffing. Well, now that they were best mates with Karen, they'd soon figure out the truth – that I was light years away from being the person they thought I was. Because Karen was sure to fill them in on a few things, wasn't she?

I saw Abby's round face, crinkling up in confusion. *Just don't let her get to you. Why do you let her get to you so much?* Ha, easy for her to say! Miss Confident. Miss Bolshy Goth Maiden.

I cringed, remembering the worst time of all – Karen's voice ringing around the tiled walls of the changing rooms as she read my notebook, while I huddled by the lockers, trying to hide, trying to disappear. A sickening flush raced over me, remembering how everyone had laughed.

It had all been Abby's fault, in a way, that was the *really* ironic thing. Because if I had never been friends with her, Karen wouldn't even have noticed me.

I buried my face in Pippin's fur until he meowed and twisted away. Wiping my hand across my eyes, I slowly opened my desk drawer. I took the dragon out from its hiding place, and ran my fingers over its spiny wings.

Oh, Abby, I miss you so much! I miss being friends with you. I'm sorry, I'm really sorry; I just couldn't take it any more. But it's all gone wrong anyway, somehow.

So what are you going to do about it? asked the tiny dragon's eyes.

Day Eight

'My god, poor Ann,' murmured Jenny for about the thousandth time, staring at the paper.

'Is that the story about *Crimewatch*?' Dad glanced up from where he was sitting on the floor with his cup of coffee.

We were all sprawled around in the lounge, finishing up our 'Townsend Traditional Sunday Brunch.' Well, it's 'traditional' whenever Dad decides he feels like cooking it. I think he thought he was cheering me up, having it today.

Jenny sighed, snapping out the newspaper and folding it over. 'Hundreds of calls, and not one that's come to anything so far.'

'Come to what?' Nat's eyes were wide. I wasn't sure what Jenny had told her about Abby – something suitably non-traumatic, probably, like Abby was off on holiday and was just a *tiny* bit late coming home – but she was always hinting about, trying to get more details.

'Nothing – finish your sausage,' ordered Dad. Nat made a face, picking at the remains of her breakfast.

I tried to take another bite of toast, and then put it down. 'So – so no one else saw her, then? After I did?'

Dad grimaced and patted my arm, leaning across the coffee table. 'Someone might still come forward with something definite, love – the show only aired a few days ago. Or maybe the police just aren't releasing everything they know to the press.'

'Oh, absolutely,' put in Jenny quickly, looking worried. She was obviously remembering that she was a child-psychologist in training, and that doom and gloom weren't really the way to go.

Nat was wide-eyed, desperate to know what was going on. I looked down, thinking that doom and gloom felt more realistic, actually.

Suddenly Dad jumped up, brushing crumbs from his trousers. 'Right, enough of this – what do you say we all go out and do something? Go see a National Trust place, enjoy the sunshine.'

'Yeah!' yelped Nat, wolfing down her last bite of sausage.

A look of consternation crossed Jenny's face. 'Oh, but I've got homework to do.'

'It's just for an afternoon.'

Jenny stood up too, and started piling our breakfast things onto the big wooden tray. The juice glasses clinked together. 'No, really, I'm afraid I can't . . . take Emma and Natalie, though.'

'Oh, come on, Jen. It's a gorgeous day—'

'Tom, *I've got homework*. It's due tomorrow; I need to get it done. This is important to me, all right?' She turned and carried the tray into the kitchen, her curly hair bouncing against the old black cardigan she wore.

Shaking his head, Dad let out a short breath and swung Nat up in his arms, perching her on his shoulders. She shrieked, clutching his neck and giggling. He glanced at me. 'What about you, Emma? Are you up for it?'

It actually sounded tempting; how sad is that? Wandering around an old manor house with my dad and Nat, peering at dusty furniture.

I shook my head. 'No, thanks. There's something else I need to do today.'

I started out with about a hundred posters, along with a box of plastic sleeves I bought at the stationery store. And a staple gun I nicked from Dad's toolbox, and a roll of masking tape and a pair of scissors. My carrier bag dragged at my shoulder like I was carrying a load of cement.

Jenny had looked like she was going to cry when she found out what I was doing. Not that I had wanted to tell her; she caught me coming downstairs with the posters. At first she wanted to help, but finally she settled for giving me a lift into town, saying that she'd pick me up at four o'clock.

My bag became lighter after I had gone to a few dozen shops, asking if I could put up posters of Abby in their window. Everyone was incredibly nice, practically falling over themselves to say yes. The worst part was that they all acted like I was a complete saint. The woman in the shoe shop had tears in her eyes as she told me how wonderful it was of me to help the family. I felt like such a fraud, but at least I was finally doing something.

I tried not to think about what would happen if Karen saw me.

Around two o'clock, I came to a shop near the library that had only opened the year before. The front of it was just a bare metal door, with THE DUNGEON in jagged red letters. A display window to the left had a full-sized Darth Vader, and an arrangement of anime comics.

I had longed to take a look inside ever since it opened, to be honest, but I knew Jo and Debbie wouldn't be interested. So I hadn't been, either. The three of us had passed by the shop loads of times, laughing about the sort of saddos who might shop there.

I pushed open the door and went in.

The walls were stone-clad, like a real dungeon, with metal stairs curving downwards. My footsteps rang against them as I descended into a brightly-lit room. Shining cases of figurines stood lit up like displays of diamonds, and there were shelves and shelves of books.

I stopped and stared at them for a moment, thinking of the box in my wardrobe and feeling almost hungry. Emma, stop it, that's not why you're here! I took a breath and went over to the counter, where a bloke with dull black hair and a straggly goatee was reading a magazine.

'Is it OK if I put this up somewhere?' I showed him the poster of Abby.

His stubbly face twisted in concern. 'Oh, right . . . we've already got one, actually.' He pointed to the wall beside one of the bookshelves. Abby's face looked out at the shop, smiling.

The guy rubbed his chin, staring at it. 'Really sad; she's in here all the time.'

I tucked the poster back in my bag. As I was looking down, I said, 'Um – what sort of things does she usually look at? I mean, what sort of books, or whatever?'

'D&D, mostly.' He nodded at the gleaming shelves against the opposite wall, where a boy in black jeans stood looking through the titles. 'She was really into gaming . . . I mean, *is* really into. Hopefully.'

My stomach jerked as I realized what he meant. 'Thanks,' I managed.

And then, instead of leaving, for some reason I found myself going over to the D&D section.

It was incredible. There were *hundreds* of books there, all of them tall and shining, filled with the same glossy, gorgeous artwork that Abby's *Monster Manual* had had.

I pulled out the *New Player's Handbook*, and looked at the table of contents. *How to Create Your Character . . . Actions in Combat . . . Casting Spells . . .*

I was reading about the different deities, completely engrossed, when the boy who had been standing there reached for a book in front of me. 'Excuse me.'

'Sorry.' I glanced up, and both of us froze.

It was the boy with the pierced eyebrow from Sheila's house.

'Oh—' I started to say hi, and stopped. Like he'd want to talk to me after everything he had probably heard from Sheila! My neck began to burn as I fumbled to put the book back on the shelf.

'Hang on – you're Emma, right?'

'*Yes*, I'm Emma.' The book completely wasn't co-operating. The space it had come out of seemed to have shrunk or something.

'What are you doing in here?' He was wearing a T-shirt that was like a tie-dye, only it was all in greys and blacks. And had skulls on it.

My cheeks were sizzling now, too. 'I'm just putting up posters, that's all. Don't worry, I'm leaving.' I finally managed to shove the book back into place, and grabbed for the bag at my feet.

'Hey, hang on, don't rush off! I didn't know you were into this stuff, that's all. Are you?'

Clutching my bag, I paused and looked at him. He was a couple of inches taller than me, with light bluish-green eyes and a nice face. Like someone you could talk to. And I slowly realized that he wasn't being snide; he was honestly asking.

I lowered my bag. 'No, not really. But Abby – mentioned it to me. Well, you know. And I was just curious.'

I was trying not to stare at his pierced eyebrow. It had a little silver hoop through it. I wondered if it ever got caught on things.

'Right . . .' Flipping his blond hair out of his eyes, he pulled out the book I had been looking at. 'Well, this is sort of the basic book if you wanted to get started. Are you into fantasy at all?'

I hesitated, and then glanced at him again. 'Yeah, I am,' I admitted. 'Well, more science-fiction, actually.'

'Oh, yeah?' His eyes lit up. 'There's some games that are sci-fi based, you know – like Cyberpunk and SLA, and then there's one based on *Star Wars*.'

'*Really?* I love *Star Wars!*'

He grinned. 'Original, or new three?'

'Oh, both – but the first new one was sort of lame. "Can Anakin win the big race and save the day?" Nowhere near as classic as the originals.'

'Yeah, no way. Jar-Jar Binks completely sucked . . .' He opened the *New Player's Handbook*. 'Anyway, it's really easy. You create a character for yourself – see, this chapter explains all about it – and then when you start to play, a games master basically just tells a story. And you and the other players decide what's going to happen in it, by the way you play your character and the choices you make.'

'It's like those *Choose Your Own Adventure* books!' I stood looking over his arm. There was an illustration of a knight with his helmet off, looking weary.

'Yeah, sort of . . .' He turned the page. 'Only there's a lot more rules, and you can cast spells and things. And anything can happen; you're not just limited to a couple of possibilities.'

'Hey, look at this, you can play an elf!' I sounded all burbly and excited, and I snapped my mouth shut as confusion swamped through me. I mean, A, what was I even doing here, and B, *what* was going on?

I reached for my bag again.

The boy's eyes widened. 'What's wrong?'

'Look, I don't even know your name. And – and you're a friend of *Sheila's*; you're supposed to hate me.'

His mouth lifted in a puzzled smile. 'I'm John Kazinski, but everyone calls me Ski. Why should I hate you?'

'Because of what happened between me and Abby.' My voice shook. Did I have to spell it *out* for him?

Ski shrugged, looking down at the book again. 'I don't know what *did* happen, only what Sheila said. And I think she's sort of jealous of you, actually.'

My jaw hit the floor with a thud. 'Jealous of *me*? Why?'

'I don't know. Because Abby talks about you a lot, I guess.'

I bit my lip. Oh, Abby. Suddenly feeling as weary as the knight in the drawing, I stared down at the carpet.

'Um . . . I don't even know how Abby got to be friends with all of you,' I said finally. 'Do you all go to Balden Comp?'

Ski shook his head. 'Wilkinson's. Year Ten.'

My eyebrows shot up. Wilkinson's is a private arts school; the sort of place I'd love to go if I had any actual talent. You have to be seriously good to get in, though. I wondered nastily what *Sheila's* great talent was.

'So how did you meet Abby?'

He shrugged. 'Last year Sheila's family moved the next street down from Abby, and they got to be friends. And Sheila's house is sort of central to where everyone

live__ere to play. Abby's really into
D&_He trailed off, swallowing.

'ith neither of us knowing
_ked; he shut the book and
_. 'I hate, I really *hate* not
her. Not even knowing

_ing to cry. 'Me too,'

'Ha__ you hear_ about the c__dlelight vigil?' He
could see from my expression that I hadn't. 'The
Ryzners' church is organizing it. It's tomorrow night,
in War Memorial Park. Everyone's supposed to bring
a candle and – you know, pray for Abby's safe return.
All her friends are going.'

Tomorrow night. Monday. That was when Debbie
had asked me over, along with her new friend Karen.
The scene in the café swept over me again, leaving
me confused and miserable.

I nodded. 'Yeah, I'll – I'll probably go.'

Ski smiled slightly. 'Really? That's great.'

I must have looked confused, because he flushed.
'I mean – well, it would be good to talk more, if . . .'
Now *his* cheeks were on fire. 'Anyway, I'd better get
home. See you tomorrow, maybe.' He took off,
hunched into his black jeans jacket.

Before I left, I bought the D&D book.

lives, so we'd all go there to play. Abby's really into D&D. I mean, she . . .' He trailed off, swallowing.

There was a pause, with neither of us knowing what to say. Ski's throat worked; he shut the book and shoved it back onto the shelf. 'I hate, I really *hate* not knowing what's happened to her. Not even knowing if she's alive or not.'

I had to look away, or I was going to cry. 'Me too,' I whispered.

'Have you heard about the candlelight vigil?' He could see from my expression that I hadn't. 'The Ryzners' church is organizing it. It's tomorrow night, in War Memorial Park. Everyone's supposed to bring a candle and – you know, pray for Abby's safe return. All her friends are going.'

Tomorrow night. Monday. That was when Debbie had asked me over, along with her new friend Karen. The scene in the café swept over me again, leaving me confused and miserable.

I nodded. 'Yeah, I'll – I'll probably go.'

Ski smiled slightly. 'Really? That's great.'

I must have looked confused, because he flushed. 'I mean – well, it would be good to talk more, if . . .' Now *his* cheeks were on fire. 'Anyway, I'd better get home. See you tomorrow, maybe.' He took off, hunched into his black jeans jacket.

Before I left, I bought the D&D book.

Day Nine

When I walked into school that morning, everything had changed. Suddenly I wasn't just Ems any more, the tall one with streaks in her hair – now everyone knew about Friday night's *Crimewatch,* and that I was the last person who had seen Abby. And they were gawping at me as if I had walked into school without my top on.

Whispers floated in my wake as I went into the main building. God, it was like being back at Balden! No, it's not. Calm, Emma, calm. No one's out to get you. Look, do you see Karen anywhere? No.

I didn't see Jo and Debbie anywhere, either. Which wasn't surprising, since I had gone in early on purpose, to avoid them. My throat tightened, thinking of the café. And they were supposed to be my friends!

Steering well clear of the trophy case, I went out to the inner courtyard, which is where the Year Tens usually hang out before class. Leaning against the rough brick wall, I closed my eyes and let the sun bathe my face like a warm flannel.

'Ems?'

My eyes flew open. It was this Year Ten girl with bright ginger hair – Sara something. She touched my arm, looking anxious.

'Ems, I saw you on TV Friday night . . . are you OK?'

'I— Oh, sure, I guess so.'

'It's so sad . . . you must be really scared for her.'

She didn't have to say Abby's name. I nodded, wrapping my arms around myself.

Three more girls came over. 'Ems, you poor thing . . .' Suddenly I was the centre of a small crowd. Girls I hardly knew were pressing close around me, squeezing my arm and even hugging me.

'I'm fine.' I wiped at my eyes, being careful of my mascara and trying to laugh. 'Really, I'm fine.'

Sara smiled sadly at me. 'Oh, Ems . . . you don't have to pretend.'

I just looked at her. I couldn't say anything. Wouldn't it be nice if she were right?

The candles in War Memorial Park that night were hundreds of flickering stars, each one lighting a worried face. TV cameras crouched on the sidelines as more people trickled in through the park gates, silently joining the others. Everyone stood hushed, waiting. On the bandstand at the park's centre, a vicar stood talking with Abby's family.

Jenny and I edged our way through the crowd. I gulped when I saw the Ryzners. Would they even want me to be there? My stepmother touched my shoulder.

'Where do you want to stand?' she whispered. 'Do

you want to get up front, and say something to the Ryzners?'

I shook my head quickly.

'Well, let's get just a bit closer, then,' she said. We made our way towards the bandstand, pushing through the crowd as politely as possible. Before I realized it, we had practically walked right into Sheila and the others. Rob, looking gangly and gaunt in his black trenchcoat. Tall, heavy-set Gail in a velvet Goth dress. Ski.

'Oh!' Sheila and I stared at each other. She was holding a candle, tears streaming down her snub-nosed face. She looked so vulnerable, her spiky hair almost child-like.

Coming up behind me, Jenny handed me a candle from her bag. 'Is here OK?' she whispered. I nodded. The candle felt slick against my hands.

Ski's eyes were red. He leaned over and lit my candle from his, his fingers brushing against mine as the gradual golden glow took hold. I tried to smile at him, but I couldn't.

I looked at Sheila. She was staring at me like she had never seen me before.

'Do you – do you mind if I stand here?' I whispered to her.

She shook her head, and then looked away, wiping her eyes. I clutched my candle. I couldn't see the Ryzners through the crowd from here, and I was glad.

A crackling came from the microphone, and suddenly the vicar's voice boomed out over us, sounding gentle even though it was so loud.

'It is difficult to know what to say at a time like this, when hope is hard to come by, yet must be held on to. We are all touched by the fearful uncertainties of Abby's disappearance. It is at times like these that we realize the reality of community; the reality that we are all bound together, and that the disappearance of one child affects us all.'

A rock lodged in my chest. Jenny stared up at the bandstand, her face streaked with tears.

'Dear Lord, please keep Abby safe. If she is alive, then help her find her way home . . .'

There was a rustling beside me as Rob put his arm around Sheila, who was sobbing. On her other side, Gail put an arm around her too, and then suddenly turned and drew me and Ski into it, making a circle.

We pressed together as the vicar's words went on. I think all of us were crying by then. Slowly, Ski held his candle out into the middle of the circle. The rest of us did, too, holding our candles together so that they almost made a single flame.

I screwed my eyes shut, feeling the warmth of the others and trying not to sob.

Abby, please, please, be all right.

Afterwards, when the crowd started breaking up and the sea of candles was drifting towards the entrance, I saw the Ryzners again, talking to the vicar on the grass. Sheila and the others hurried over to them, hugging, offering comfort.

'No!' I tugged at Jenny's sleeve when she started to join them. 'No – Jenny, please, let's just go home.'

Day Ten

'. . . Police say they cannot discount the possibility that
Abby went off with someone she knew, as any struggle
would have been noticed by passers-by . . . meanwhile,
huge photos of Abby have been put on the sides of
lorries, in the hope that they will jog memories.'
Local news broadcast, Tuesday 14th September

I sat in English class leaning my head on my hand,
staring down at my exercise book without seeing it.
The vigil wouldn't leave my mind. I kept seeing the
hundreds of flickering candles, like fairy lights, and
hearing the vicar's words about holding on to hope.
Did he know how incredibly *difficult* it was, though?

At the front of the room, Mrs Patel was going on
about that passage in *Beowulf* where he hacks Grendel's
mother to bits.

'So hang on, miss,' said Scott Price. 'You have this
poor monster, grieving because this bloke's *already*
killed her son, and now—'

Suddenly a piercing bell tore through the lesson.
Everyone jumped, except Mrs Patel, who suddenly

turned brusque and businesslike. 'Fire drill! Everyone out, quickly now. Don't stop to get your things, just go!'

Everyone ignored her, scooping up their bags as they filed out of the room. Doors were popping open all up and down the corridor as people streamed out. The alarm kept bleating, pulsing around us.

Outside on the front lawn, teachers were shouting and herding everyone about. 'Year Nine, get in your form rooms!' shrieked Mrs Newman, our form head. 'Alphabetical order, quickly, quickly!'

I had forgotten about that bit of the fire drill. Suddenly I felt like I had just gained twenty stone. Debbie's surname was Traner. Mine was Townsend.

'Hi.' I tried to smile as I took my place beside her in the line, just as if I hadn't been avoiding her and Jo at all this week – saying I had to go to the library for lunch yesterday, rushing into classes late so I didn't have to sit with them.

'Hi, Ems.' Debbie's smile was uncertain.

Mrs Newman paced up and down the line, ticking off names. 'Holman, Kate – where are you, Kate? Get in *line*, you silly girl, hurry now! If there were a fire you'd be crisped by now. Ingram, Matthew—'

'How was babysitting last night?' asked Debbie suddenly.

That's what I had told her I was doing last night, the reason why I couldn't go over to her house with Jo. I lifted a shoulder. 'OK, I guess.'

She watched Mrs Newman for a second, and then

glanced back at me, her mouth tense. 'Look, Ems . . .
my dad saw you on TV. At the vigil, I mean.'

I winced. But why should *I* feel guilty? She and Jo
were the ones who were too busy cosying up to Karen
to notice the first thing about how I felt!

'Why did you lie to us about it?'

'I don't have to tell you everything I do, do I?'

'No, but—'

I spoke wildly, flinging the words out. 'Look, I just
need some time to myself, OK? I mean, I've been really
upset about Abby, and . . .' I stopped and folded my
arms over my chest, watching the long lines being
counted like it was totally fascinating.

'And what?' Her green eyes looked hurt, angry.

I shrugged, keeping my gaze on the counting.

Suddenly the alarm stopped, like someone turning
off a tap of noise. Mrs Newman clapped her hands.
'Right, well done, everyone. Back inside, now!' The
form groups drifted towards the school, laughing and
shouting to each other.

'So . . . you don't want to be friends any more? Is
that it? Or what?' Debbie's voice sounded like a rubber
band about to snap.

'Don't be so dramatic. I didn't say that.' I grabbed
up my rucksack from the ground.

Jo appeared. A worried frown creased her face as
she took in our expressions. 'Um . . . is everything OK?'

Why don't you ask your new friend, Karen?

'Everything's just great,' I said.

Debbie let out a short breath. 'Ems, you're being
really—'

'Really *what?*'

'I don't know!' snapped Debbie. 'But I'm getting bloody sick of it! You've been completely avoiding us for days, and acting like we can't possibly understand anything, and—'

'So what? Why can't you just leave me alone, the pair of you!'

Jo's eyes were wide. 'Ems, what—'

'Just *go away!* Leave me alone!'

Debbie's chin jerked up. 'Fine, if that's how you want it. Come on, Jo.' She took Jo's arm, and they started off across the grass. Jo glanced back at me before their heads drew close together, talking.

My head swirled hotly. But I had every reason to be less than thrilled with them, didn't I? And it wasn't like they'd still *want* to be my friends, once they'd had a few conversations with Karen.

I walked alone across the playing-fields, remembering that day in the girls' changing rooms. Remembering a hundred other days. *Don't you dare go crying to Mrs Evans, Freak, or you'll wish you were dead . . . Ooh, look, Freaky's fallen down again! . . . Aw, poor widdle Freak – it's all just too much for her. Boo-hoo-hoo.*

What would Jo and Debbie think when they found out? Stupid question! What would *anyone* think, if they found out someone they knew had been such a pathetic kick-bag? A headache spiked my temples. I scanned the crowd of girls ahead of me and watched Jo and Debbie go up the stairs into school together. And decided that I was relieved to be rid of them.

* * *

'Where's Nat?' I asked when I got home.

Jenny glanced up from her maths book. 'At her swimming lesson . . . it's Tuesday.'

'Oh. Right.' I wasn't really hungry, but I took an apple from the fruit bowl and crunched into it, feeling like a piece of string that's fraying at the ends. What was the use of having a little sister if she wasn't around to distract you?

So I went into Dad's study to use his computer, perching on the edge of his black leather desk chair and logging onto the Internet. Moving the mouse, I clicked 'TeenzOwn' from my favourite places folder.

Not that it's one of my favourite places – it's all bright colours and bubble-shaped letters, like they think teenagers are just the tiniest bit thick – but it's one of the only sites I'm allowed on . And I really felt like an hour or so of mindless clicking and reading, just then.

But I didn't get it. The first thing I saw when the website flickered onto the screen was Abby's photo. *Have you seen this girl?* It looked like a close-up of one of the holiday photos Mr Ryzner had shown me: Abby's smiling face in front of a blue, blue sky.

My throat swelled. I felt like sobbing, or punching the computer image, shattering it into oblivion. I couldn't escape it, no matter what. Abby was always there – always missing.

Suddenly all I wanted to do was talk to Mum. I dived across the desk for Dad's phone, jabbing in the international numbers. A pause, and then I heard the different-sounding ringing of an American phone, going off in an art gallery in Chicago.

'The Benson Gallery, may I help you?' The man's flat American drawl sounded artistically bored.

'Um, hi – this is Emma Townsend. Could I speak to my mother, please?' I tucked a leg under me, hugging myself with one arm.

'This is who?'

A flush galloped up my cheeks. Didn't she ever *mention* me, then? 'Emma Townsend. My mum is Rhea Antoni.'

'Oh, you want *Rhea*! Sorry, hon, I didn't understand. Rhea's out with a client; I don't expect her back for another hour or so. Do you want me to tell her you called?' The voice seemed to get more American the longer he talked, like any second now he was going to chirrup *Have a nice day!* at me.

'No, um – that's OK, I'll ring back,' I muttered.

'Try her around twelve. Bye, hon.'

I hung up, feeling like a limp balloon a week after a kids' party. Even though I knew it was pathetic of me. Mum had a job – I couldn't expect her to be there for me every second. I shouldn't even *need* her to be; I'd be fourteen in February!

But I still wanted to cry.

The phone rang suddenly, making me jump. Had Mum's boss rung her on her mobile, maybe? I snatched up the phone, leaning forward. 'Hello?'

'Hi, Emma . . . um, it's Sheila.'

It took me a second to speak. 'Oh . . . hi.'

'Look, I just wanted to say that – I'm sorry for giving you such a hard time. I wanted to tell you that at the vigil last night, but it was too . . .' Her voice dwindled

108

to nothing, and she cleared her throat. 'Anyway, I guess – I guess you care about Abby, too. So I'm sorry.'

I stared blankly at the Executive Stress-Buster toy that Dad has on his desk. 'Yeah, um . . . OK. Thanks.'

Her voice took on its usual spiky edge, like needles piercing into my ear. 'Anyway, that's really all I wanted to say. So-o . . . see you around, I guess.' *Click.*

In slow motion, I rested the phone back on its stand. I could still see Abby's face staring at me. Grabbing the mouse, I quickly closed down the computer, and let out a breath as the screen went dark.

Maybe it should have felt good to have Sheila apologize, but it didn't. It made everything worse, somehow.

'Look, who's that?' Nat bounced on my bed in her dinosaur nightgown, pointing at a picture in the *New Player's Handbook*. I was flipping slowly through it, looking at the pictures and reading bits here and there. The little dragon from Abby's room sat on the duvet beside us.

'That's . . .' I glanced at the caption. Apparently it was a half-orc, half-human warrior. 'Um, that's Gorg. He's Jasmine's personal valet. That's like a butler. So when we were summoned to her castle—'

'He answered the door!' breathed Nat. She walked the dragon over Pippin's softly snoring side. 'But with the help of our dragons . . . we will save the day!'

I fell silent, reading about the game. It was so *real*. And at the same time, it was the ultimate game of Let's Pretend. No wonder Abby loved it; it was right up her street. I turned a page, thinking about a Family Fun Fair at Clarkson Chemicals, two years ago.

The Family Fun Fair was the yearly summer torture, where Abby and I got dragged along with our dads and the rest of the families and everyone else who worked at Clarkson – hundreds of people who probably didn't even like each other at the office, but they all had to show up at the FFF and wander around naff rides together.

Abby and I had to smile while our fathers stood on the grass chatting – Abby's father at least having grasped the idea of 'casual' in his shorts and T-shirt, and mine looking as starched as usual in his chinos and polished shoes. And we had to be polite to all their colleagues, who'd pop up and say things like, 'Why, is this really Little Emma! You'll have to watch out, love, you'll be beating the boys off with a stick when you get a bit older, ho ho ho!' Then they'd all stand around and talk about their dreary jobs for a hundred years.

Finally the oldies would suss that Abby and I were frothing with boredom, and let us go off and experience the joy of the fair. Which took about three seconds, and then we'd sneak off and explore the rest of the plant, skulking around the miles of buildings and offices.

The year just before we started Year Seven, we pretended that we were novice mages, on the run in a hostile city. It was our Esmerelda game – the one we had played for years, adding to the story until it had a whole history of its own.

'Shh!' hissed Abby. She peered around the corner of an office building, just barely poking her nose out. And she wasn't wearing cut-off shorts and a T-shirt; she was wearing a long, ragged cloak, heavy with dust from many days of travel.

She shoved her hair back, dark eyes glinting with fear. 'I think the coast is clear . . . do you have the spell ready, just in case?'

'I think so,' I whispered back, pressing tight against the wall. 'But you know we've never used it before – the power may be too much for us—'

'We have no choice; we have to find the scroll! Now run!'

It sounds pretty cringe-worthy, but it *wasn't,* it was the most fantastic fun. Abby always threw herself right into any pretend game, playing like it was for real.

So we really were mages, for a couple of hours that day. And we found the scroll in the end – an old paper napkin – and managed to defeat Esmerelda the Evil Enchantress in a spell-sizzling battle that lasted for days, practically.

It was the last really good time with Abby that I could remember. I turned another page, lost in thought.

'What happens next in the game?' demanded Nat, pulling at my arm. 'What does the book say?'

'Let's see . . .' I flipped through it, pretending to read. 'Well, actually, it says – oh no! That can't be right!'

'*What?*' Her eyes were dinner-plates.

'Nat, we're in more danger than we ever knew,' I

whispered. 'Have I ever told you about an evil sorceress called – called Esmerelda?'

She shook her head, mouth slightly open.

'Well, she's even more powerful than Jasmine. She's the queen of ice and fire, and we thought we had defeated her years ago . . . but it turns out that Jasmine is her daughter, and now Jasmine has found her mother's old book of spells.' I could see the book as I spoke – old, cracked leather, crusted with evilly glowing rubies.

Nat hopped to the floor, clutching the green plastic straw that was her wand. 'We'll have to go after her!'

'But remember, she escaped from us last time, and we don't know where she is . . . we'll have to travel to – to the plains of Ganet, and consult with the wizards there.'

We looked gravely at each other. Nat nodded, and I motioned for her to sit beside me. She climbed back up on the bed. 'Right, just close your eyes, and we'll be there . . .'

There was a sudden knock on my door. 'What?' I called, flopping quickly across the bed so that I was lying on top of the dragon. Its wings dug into my ribcage.

Dad stuck his head in. 'So this is where everyone's hiding! Nat, it's almost time for bed. And how's the homework coming along, Emma?'

'I haven't exactly started yet . . .' I tried to casually shove the *New Player's Handbook* under a pillow. It was a bit difficult to be casual about it, since I was lying down and the pillow was at the opposite end of the bed.

Predictably, Dad came into the room. 'I know it's hard, love, but you can't let yourself get behind. What's that you're looking at?'

He picked up the book. Little lines sprouted on his forehead as he flipped through it. 'What *is* this?'

'Just a D&D book. I, um, bought it at this shop in town.' I felt Nat's hand digging under my side, and then the dragon was gone. I sat up in relief and smiled at her, and she winked solemnly back. She's pretty cool sometimes, for a six-year-old.

Dad looked up. 'What's D&D, then?' So I had to explain about Dungeons and Dragons, and it was completely painful. *See, you pretend to be an elf, and . . .*

His eyebrows drew together as I spoke. 'Aren't you a bit old for all this?'

'Well – no, not really. I mean, I think quite old people play it, actually. Adults.'

Dad shrugged, and tossed the book onto the bed. It landed with a soft *plump* beside me. 'Well, whatever keeps you happy. Looks a bit odd to me. Come on now, Nat, time for bed.'

The word kicked me in the stomach. Odd. Thanks, Dad.

As Nat scrambled off the bed, she pressed the dragon into my hand, smiling angelically. (I swear she has a future as a con artist.) ''Night, Emma.'

''Night, Nat,' I murmured back. I watched her leave the room with Dad, and clutched the tiny statue, running my thumb over the scales on its neck. It felt like a lifeline – but a lifeline to what? Being *odd* all my life?

I pulled my knees up to my chest and looked at my wardrobe, thinking of the box. Of the notebook, filled with pages and pages of writing. And Karen's voice, laughing as she read – *'Only magic can save us now, my friend! Ooh, magic-wagic!'*

Odd was just an adult word for *freak*, wasn't it?

Finally I picked the book up and started reading again. And slowly, I fell back into it, until the only sound was the soft turning of pages.

A sharp noise clapped through the room, and I jolted upright. Blearily, I realized that I had fallen asleep, and dropped the book on the floor. I blinked at the clock. It was almost eleven.

I rolled onto my stomach to grab the book from where it lay splayed on the carpet – and stopped. There was a neon-green flier beside it; it must have been tucked into the book. I picked it up, stretching my fingers to grasp it.

Annual Gaming Convention, November 15–17, Manchester University

- ***Table gaming*** – *D20 Modern, D&D classic, Star Wars, Dark Sun, SLA, Cyberpunk, Cthulu, etc. etc.!*
- ***Live action games*** – *Night of the Dead, Hero, Vampire, Goth*
  - *Massive trade hall*
    - *AND MORE!*

Live action. But . . . hadn't Abby mentioned that on the bus? I sat up slowly on the bed, staring at the flier as phrases whirled around me, hitting me like hailstones.

We've been doing table gaming, but that's sort of boring . . . I'm going to get them into live action, not that they know it yet . . . You want to come along this afternoon, then? Should be almost as much fun . . .

I gripped the flier, remembering how stunned I had been when the police first started questioning me, how I had struggled to remember what Abby had said. And now, eleven days later, the exact words she had used had come flooding back. *Live action.*

But what was it that I was remembering? What *was* a live action game, anyway?

Dad. I had to find Dad; I had to tell someone! I scrambled off the bed and lunged into the corridor, starting quickly down the stairs. When I was halfway down, I heard my name, and froze.

'I suppose I'm just a bit worried about it, that's all,' said Dad's voice. 'I mean, she was into all that fantasy stuff with Abby, but she really seemed to have matured so much this last year at St Sebastian's. Now it's like she's harking back or something, buying that book . . .'

My pulse hammered. I pressed against the wall, listening.

Jenny's voice floated up. 'A bit of regression, maybe? I mean, nothing serious, I'm sure, but she must want to retreat back to a safer time, with all that's going on. It's all very frightening, Tom, for her especially.'

She sounded so revoltingly *earnest,* so chuffed that Dad was even asking her opinion. The future child psychologist in action.

Dad sighed. 'Yes, I know she must be terrified by all this . . . what can we do, though?'

I heard what sounded like a coffee cup being put down. 'Well, counselling might be an idea. Just to help her over this time – give her some skills to cope.'

I stiffened against the wall. No *way.* That was apparently Dad's reaction too, because Jenny said edgily, 'Tom, it's a totally common thing . . . good grief, I've had counselling myself.'

I could just picture Dad's grimace. 'Yes, well . . . it's an option to keep in mind, I suppose. But for now, we'll just keep an eye on her, shall we? See that she doesn't start to – retreat too much into this fantasy stuff, or act odd in other ways.'

'And I'll see if she wants to talk about things . . . maybe have a word with her tomorrow.'

Oh, will you? I flushed, shaking with shame and anger. It was like I had let Dad down by not being as fantastically mature as he had thought. I wanted to burst downstairs and scream at them that they didn't know anything, that half the time I had been acting this last year, *acting,* so that I didn't get slaughtered at my new school for being – what was the word? Oh yes, *odd.*

My fingernails bit into my palms, and suddenly I was near tears. The thought of trying to explain to Dad about the flier made my stomach jerk. I couldn't do it, not now.

I moved back up the stairs, placing my feet carefully on the carpet so they wouldn't hear me.

When I eventually eased away into sleep that night, Abby and the game drifted around in my head like smoke. Abby was wearing a cloak, slipping through the night with a tiger-eye necklace in her hand.

And she didn't know that Esmerelda was hiding just around the next corner, waiting for her.

Day Eleven

Sheila's face slackened as she opened her front door and saw me standing there. 'Oh. What do you want?' She crossed her skinny arms across her chest.

'Can I talk to you?' I burst out. 'It's important.'

Her eyebrows almost disappeared under her spiky fringe. She shrugged, and stood back to let me in. 'Yeah, I guess. Whatever.'

In the lounge, a boy of about seventeen was sprawled in front of a wide-screen TV, where large American blokes in masks were wrestling each other. 'Hold on, folks . . . YES! The Muskrat strikes again!' The TV crowd roared, '*Musk-rat! Musk-rat!*'

And Dad thinks *I'm* odd.

The boy and Sheila completely ignored each other as we passed through the lounge. Sheila grabbed a pair of Cokes from the fridge and we went up to her room, stepping over a fat black Labrador on the way.

'His name is Fred,' said Sheila over her shoulder as we went into her room. 'We've had him since I was about two . . . he's useless; all he ever does is drool.'

I assumed she was talking about the dog, not the boy.

'Yeah, I've got a cat like that . . .' I tapered off, trying to get my head around the fact that we were actually having a civil conversation. It felt unnatural.

Sheila handed me one of the Cokes and sat down at her desk. I sank onto her bed, looking around the room. And somehow I wanted to prolong being friendly, so I nodded at this fantastic poster on her wall – a mage on a cliff, with lightning streaming around him – and said, 'That's really great . . . where did you get it?'

Sheila glanced at it. 'Yeah, my Art teacher thought it was OK . . . it was in the Art Show last year.'

I thought she had *bought* it! I popped open my Coke, feeling completely inadequate. 'Um . . . it's fantastic.'

'Thanks.' She squinted sceptically at it. 'I'm more into anime now. So's Gail . . . that's how we all met, in fact – the four of us. We have Art together.'

'Ski's an artist?'

She slid a sidelong glance at me. 'Yeah, that's right. He's really into graphic comics. Design, that sort of thing. Why?'

'Just wondering.' I took a quick gulp of Coke to hide my reddening face.

Sheila smiled knowingly, straightening out a paper clip. 'That's funny; he was asking about you, too. On and on. Goth Girl and I were about to gag him to shut him up.'

I froze. 'Goth—'

'Gail.' Sheila gave me a strange look. 'She's the original Goth Girl, or haven't you noticed?'

'It's just that—' I took a breath. 'Well, that's what they call Abby at Balden. One of the things. Only they're not kidding.'

The desk chair squeaked as Sheila pulled a knee up to her chest. 'She never told me that. She told me enough, though. They sound like a bunch of stuck-up cows at that school.'

'Some of them really are. Like Karen Stipp and them.' Glancing down at my forest green uniform, I thought about how I had just skipped off and left Abby to fend for herself. My mouth tightened, thinking about it. I mean, she had always claimed not to care about Karen, but what if she really did? What if *she'd* been acting, too?

I could feel Sheila's eyes on me, and knew that she was dying to ask what had happened. I rested the Coke on a pink beaded drink-mat that sat on her bedside table.

'Look, the reason I came here . . . I saw this flier about a D&D convention, and it mentioned live action games. And it reminded me that that's what Abby was talking about on the bus.'

There was a flash of blue as Sheila's eyes widened. 'What exactly did she say?'

'That – table gaming was starting to get boring, and the game *she* was going to run would be live action.'

Sheila slumped back in her chair, gaping at me like I had just started chanting ancient Latin. 'What, the game we were going to play *that night*?'

My heart racketed against my ribs. 'That's what it sounded like. What does it mean, anyway?'

'Um . . . well, it's when you play a game outside, in a real setting – like, if the game's set in the woods, then you actually go play it in the woods, acting it out. Emma, are you *sure* she said that?'

'Yes, I'm sure! I just didn't know what it meant at first, so it didn't really sink in.'

'But . . .' Sheila's mouth pursed. 'Did she say where we were supposed to go to play it?'

'No, but she asked me if I wanted to play that night, and when I said no, she asked me along for that afternoon. She said it should be almost as much fun. Sheila, I thought she was inviting me to her *house!*'

Sheila shook her head slowly. 'No, I bet she was asking you along somewhere else, to help set up the game . . . and it wouldn't have been at her house, because we were supposed to all meet *here* that night.' She stopped suddenly, pressing a fist against her mouth.

'What?'

'I just thought – she knows my mum does line dancing Saturday nights! She knew we could leave the house if we met here – so if she was talking about live action, then she *definitely* must have been setting up a game somewhere else for us to play, and I bet that's where she was going when you saw her on the bus!'

Electricity shot through me, lifting the hair from my head. We stared at each other. I knew we were both thinking the same thing: Abby going to the woods or something. By herself.

'And I bet that's what the tiger-eye necklace was for,' I managed. 'Like, for treasure . . . something real for you to find at the end of the game.'

Sheila's pointed face had turned fish-belly pale. 'Emma, we've got to go to the police. We've got to tell them all of this.'

'Yeah, you're right.' I fumbled to get my mobile out of my bag. 'Do you reckon I should just dial 999, or—'

'No, we have to go there!' Exploding from her desk, Sheila snatched up a bus pass from her dresser and shoved it in her pocket.

'*Go* there?'

'Emma, this is urgent! We can't just *ring* – come on, they're going to want to talk to you in person anyway, aren't they? And the fastest way for that to happen is if we just *go there, now.*'

She stood by her door with her hands on her hips, looking like an outraged blond ferret.

I tried not to think about the fact that it was already after half four, and that I had told Jenny I was going to a Book Club meeting after school. I stood up and grabbed my things. 'OK . . . you're right.'

A few minutes later, we were running for the bus.

The police department was in the Civic Building just beside the town centre – a tall, concrete office block that looked like a prison. All it needed were coils of barbed wire surrounding it.

Even Sheila looked a bit daunted as we got closer. She took a breath and shoved open the door. 'Come on.'

I followed right behind her, my pulse drumming in my ears.

PC Lavine was there when we asked for her, which was a complete relief. And she was as nice as I remembered. She took us into a private office, and sat with us on a small sofa as I repeated what Abby had said, and explained how I had remembered it the night before.

'See, live action games are different from table games,' Sheila broke in.

PC Lavine had pulled out a small notebook, and was writing in it with a blue Biro. She glanced up. 'Yes, I know . . . we've had a D&D expert in.'

Goatee-guy from the Dungeon flashed into my mind.

'Oh.' Sheila looked a bit deflated. 'Well, anyway, we don't think she was going home that day, since the game was going to be live action . . . she must have been going somewhere to set it up for that night.'

'Right, I see.' Frowning, PC Lavine went over it again with us, asking loads of questions. What were the exact words Abby had used, could I recall? Had Abby ever mentioned live action gaming before? Did we have any idea at all where she might have gone to set up a game?

Sheila and I looked at each other on that last one, shaking our heads. I saw the same blankness on her face that I felt on mine.

Finally PC Lavine nodded, and snapped the cap back on her Biro.

'Right . . . wait here a moment, girls, I want to show you something.' She came back a few seconds later with a bulging file, and handed us some stapled-together sheets of paper. 'This is the game we think Abby wrote for you and your friends to play, Sheila. We found it on the hard drive of her family's computer; she printed a copy of it off the day she disappeared.'

Sheila and I pressed together on the sagging sofa, looking down at the game.

Esmerelda's Dungeon
An adventure for a party of four, with experience level five.

PC Lavine sat down and placed the heaving file on the desk. 'Have a quick read of it, OK? See if it rings any bells as to where she might have been planning to play it.'

I was still gawking at the title. How could she have made this into an *Esmerelda* game? Esmerelda was ours!

Gripping the paper, I started to read. *The Eye of Fire, a talisman of great power, has been stolen by the evil enchantress Esmerelda. A party of four adventurers have been hired to get the Eye back. After a long journey, and many hardships, they have managed to chase Esmerelda down into the dungeons under her castle. It is here that our story begins.*

So she hadn't used the stories we created together after all; she had just taken the name Esmerelda. But it still felt like a complete betrayal.

I started to turn the page. Sheila's hand slapped it down again. 'Do you mind? I'm not finished yet.'

But when she turned the page, the story part had ended. There was some description, but mostly it was stuff like this:

If the party advance without checking for/finding traps, poison spores will be released and they will lose one const. pt per round until antidote is found.

If the party decide to explore Secret Chambers 1 or 2, they find nothing. Secret Chamber 3 is open, and has 20 gp.

Pages of that sort of thing, absolute pages of it. Sheila nodded seriously as she read, like it made perfect sense to her. I struggled on, trying to picture what the actual game might be like from all of this, but I couldn't begin to.

Finally, Sheila handed the pages back. 'Was there a map?'

PC Lavine shook her head. Her skin looked paler in the harsh office lighting, more cappuccino than milk chocolate. 'No, we haven't found one.'

'I don't know, then.' Sheila's eyebrows drew together anxiously. 'I mean, it seems really complex . . . a place with rooms and passageways and stuff. Unless we were supposed to just pretend a lot of it.'

My pulse quickened as I stared at her. Her words seemed to kick-start something in my brain; something that almost made sense, if I could just remember—

'Emma, what about you?'

It was gone. I shook my head in frustration. 'No . . . no, I don't know either.'

PC Lavine drew a little folder out of her pocket. 'Girls, look – here's my card.' She handed one to each of us. 'Give me a ring if you think of anything else, OK? Either of you, anytime. And thanks so much for coming in with this information; it could really be invaluable.'

Sheila clutched her card. 'Um – could we have a copy of Abby's game?'

The constable's sculpted eyebrows rose. 'No, I'm afraid not. I can't give out copies of evidence.'

'But – we could take it home and really study it, and—'

'I'm sorry; it's out of the question—' PC Lavine broke off as a constable with a grey moustache leaned in the doorway. From the busy office behind him, the sound of phones and conversation drifted in.

'Beth, could I have a quick word? It's about the Javez case; I've got Mrs Javez on the phone.'

PC Lavine was already starting out of the room, taking Abby's game with her. 'Just a minute, girls – I'll be back in a second to show you out,' she said over her shoulder.

Sheila and I looked at each other. Her eyes were wide and urgent, asking a question. I swallowed, and nodded. And like we had planned it for years, I moved in front of the open doorway, blocking the view as I pretended to be checking a text on my mobile. Behind me, I heard Sheila lunge for the file on the desk.

Flap, flap, flap as she rifled through it. I pressed some random buttons on my phone, trying to ignore the fact that there were police constables everywhere I looked. 'Can't you hurry?' I hissed.

'Ah *ha* – another copy!'

I glanced over my shoulder and saw Sheila turn her back to the door, folding up some pages and shoving them down her jeans. Thank god! I let out a breath and sank down onto the sofa.

PC Lavine came back just as Sheila turned around again, looking completely relaxed. 'Right, sorry about that. This way, girls.'

The five of us sat crowded around a plastic yellow table in McDonald's, looking at the crumpled pages of Abby's game. Ski sat across from me. And even though I felt horrible for thinking about it just then, I kept stealing glances at him, remembering what Sheila had said. Once I caught him looking at me, and I flushed, taking a quick sip of Sprite to hide my face.

Rob hunched over the table as he read. 'God, all these tunnels and rooms . . . where could she have had in mind for this?'

'Maybe someone's house?' Ski's blond hair fell across his face as he leaned forward, straining to read upside down. At the next table, a little kid was bopping her balloon against the wall, keeping time with some sad old tune from the eighties that was blasting from the loudspeakers.

'But it would have to be one of our houses, wouldn't it? And it wasn't,' said Gail.

Sheila had texted Gail when we left the police station, and arranged for them to meet us at the McDonald's in the town centre. And meanwhile, I had rung Jenny and told her that the Book Club meeting had been cancelled, and that I was at McDonald's with Jo and Debbie.

She had *not* been pleased.

'It looks like a really good scenario . . .' Rob flipped the stapled pages back to page one. 'I wish she had got the chance to run it for us.'

I looked at the neatly typed lines of print, and the feeling of frustration swept me again. *Why* couldn't I think of whatever it was?

'Could we . . . um, play it ourselves, maybe?' I suggested.

Instant silence as everyone stared at me.

'Why would we want to do that?' asked Sheila, wrinkling her upturned nose.

Because something about it is driving me completely mad and I don't know what. I shrugged, squeaking my straw in and out of the plastic lid. 'I don't know . . . I'd just like to play a game, and see what it's like.'

'But *this* game?' Gail's large face looked stricken, too pale under her crimson-red hair.

I swallowed. 'Yeah . . . because it's Abby's. And because . . . well, it deserves to be played. I mean, if we don't play it, who will?'

Everyone sort of winced and looked down. Finally Ski cleared his throat, and picked up the scenario, glancing through it. 'I guess I could run it as a table game. If you really want to play it, that is.'

My hair moved on my shoulders as I nodded. 'Yeah, I'd like to.'

'I would too,' said Sheila suddenly. Her earrings glinted as she glanced around at the others. 'I mean

129

– well, maybe we owe it to Abby, don't you think? To play her game? We could do it tomorrow night, at my house.'

Everyone started talking excitedly then, even Gail, their words crashing and tumbling over each other. But then it all went completely pear-shaped, because the door opened and Dad walked in.

Dad hardly said a word during the drive home. I hunched against the door, wishing that the car ride would just go on forever, that he'd suddenly take it into his head to drive to Athens or somewhere.

But instead of heading off to sunnier climes he just drove to Larkwood, and pulled up in front of our terraced house. He turned off the car, and I flinched, knowing what was coming.

'Right, Emma – what exactly is going on? Jenny said you were at McDonald's with Jo and Debbie.'

'Well – I was, only they had to go, and then I met – um, ran into Sheila and the others. You know, Sheila – from the re-enactment?'

Grim lines appeared around his mouth. 'I'm having a hard time believing that that's the entire truth, actually. Was the Book Club meeting cancelled, or not?'

I gazed down at the rough carpet on the car's floor.

'You don't know, do you? Did you even plan to go to it?'

'No,' I whispered.

'Well? Come on, out with it. What's going on?'

'I – went to the police,' I gulped out.

His eyes bulged. 'You *what?*'

So then I had to tell him the whole thing, except I didn't mention going to Sheila's house first, or that I had overheard him and Jenny talking the night before. Like I was really eager to listen to all the blustering excuses he'd come up with. *Oh, no, love, I don't think you're odd. Just regressing a teensy bit, that's all!*

Besides, he looked gobsmacked enough as it was. He had collapsed back in his seat, staring at me. 'Why on earth didn't you tell me? You didn't have to go off on your own!'

I lifted a shoulder. 'I don't know.'

'Emma, that's not good enough. You have to come to me or Jenny with this sort of thing, not go dashing off by yourself, lying to us about where you're going! Do you understand?'

I nodded, feeling miserable. Tomorrow night, what about that? I couldn't imagine asking him if I could go to Sheila's to play the game that Abby wrote.

Dad let out a short breath, tapping his fingers on the steering wheel. 'Look, Emma, I know how upset you must be about Abby. I think it might help if—'

'I'm not going to counselling!' I burst out.

His eyebrows arched. 'Who said anything about counselling?'

'I just thought—'

'Jenny's suggested it, actually.' He grimaced and loosened his tie, like the very idea choked him. 'Well, it's there as an option for us, but I think we can get through this without it, don't you? Just so long as we *talk* to each other.' He squeezed my shoulder, shaking it slightly. 'You have to trust us, Emma. OK? No more lying, no more going off on your own. Promise?'

My throat clutched up as I nodded. Looking at him, sitting there so solid in his grey suit, suddenly I wanted to burst into tears and tell him everything that I had kept secret for so long. Karen, the changing rooms – every hideous bit of it.

I licked my lips, and took a breath. 'Dad—'

He didn't hear me. He was reaching in the back seat for his briefcase. 'So those were Abby's friends, were they? That gang at McDonald's?'

I blinked. 'Oh – yeah.'

'Mm.' Dad shook his head, and his mouth twisted ironically, like – *yep, just as I thought. Weirdos.*

It felt like he had drenched me with a bucket of Arctic water. And I knew I couldn't tell him anything after all.

Jenny was 'caring and concerned' all through tea, obviously trying to draw me out. I felt like informing her that I wasn't in the mood to be practised on for her future cases, thank you very much, but I shoved the words down and played along with it.

'Yeah, I guess I should have told you both . . . I just sort of panicked, I guess.' I concentrated on cutting up my chicken.

Jenny shot Dad a pleased look. I could see them both relaxing, thinking that OK, they had had a bit of a blip on the odd-front, but now I was back to being *normal and mature* again.

'Never mind, what's done is done,' said Jenny. 'And the really important thing is that the police have the new information you gave them.'

I nodded. Swallowing a bit of chicken, I glanced across the table at Dad. 'Um, listen . . . is it OK if I go to Debbie's tomorrow night?'

He stopped eating to look at me, his eyebrows knotted together. 'No, I don't think so, Emma. It's a school night, and I'm not happy about it after what happened today.'

'But Dad, this is really important! Debbie's going to be making her outfit for the fashion contest over the weekend, so she wants Jo and me to go around for dinner tomorrow night, and then help her with the pattern and cutting out the material and all that . . . so can I go, *please*?' I held my breath.

'Oh, why not? It sounds like it would fun for her,' put in Jenny. Like we were allies as usual, ganging up on Dad. I didn't look at her.

Dad dabbed his lips with a paper napkin and sort of smiled. 'Since when can you sew?'

'Mrs Traner is going to help. Come on, Dad, please?'

'All right, I suppose it's OK. What time do they want you there?'

Thank god! I breathed out. 'Around six . . . I can just take the bus, or—'

'Don't be silly, I'll drive you.'

No-o! Never mind, stay calm; I'd figure it out later. 'OK. Thanks.'

When I went upstairs, I leaned against my door

for a long time, staring at my room and thinking that the only things in it that really had anything to do with me were my 'post-ironic' Darth Vader clock, and the dragon from Abby's room. Which wasn't even mine.

Is that sad, or what?

Day Twelve

I almost rang Dad about a dozen times from school, to tell him that the plans had changed and that I was just going home with Debbie that afternoon. But I couldn't do it; I was too afraid that he might ring Debbie's mum to check. Besides, I had forgotten to bring my D&D book with me, and didn't have a change of clothes.

We had a library period that afternoon, but I couldn't concentrate. I kept pulling books out, glancing at them and jamming them back on the shelf again. I peeked over at Jo and Debbie. They were leaning against a shelf in the paperback section, their heads bent over a Jacqueline Wilson book.

A painful twinge tugged in my chest. Maybe I was just being stupid. Maybe I should just *talk* to them.

My hands felt clammy. I rubbed them on my skirt and started slowly towards them, squeezing past a gang of boys who were clustered around the CDs. Jo and Debbie didn't see me; they were totally engrossed in the book.

But when I got closer, I saw that it wasn't the *book*

they were engrossed in at all. They were using it to hide Debbie's mobile.

'What should I say?' whispered Debbie. Her thumb was poised over the keys.

Jo's face twisted as she considered. 'How about – "Sounds great, we'll see you then. Pretty freaky, all right!"'

I stopped in my tracks as an avalanche of panic pounded over me. Karen, they were texting Karen! *What had she told them?*

Before they could look up and see me, I dashed back behind the shelf, grabbing a book and staring down at it blindly. I stood like that, completely frozen, until the bell rang.

I don't even know what I was reading.

I tried to act normal during the drive to Debbie's that night, but as we got closer and closer I felt like diving under the seat and biting off all my nails. How exactly was I going to pull this off? Sheila's house was in the exact opposite direction! Not to mention that Debbie was the last person in the universe who I wanted to see right now. Except maybe her mate, *Karen.*

Dad smiled at me as he pulled up at the kerb. 'Right, have a good time. When should I pick you up?'

I looked away, fumbling to pick up my carrier bag. It had my D&D book in it, with a jacket thrown over the top. 'Oh – that's OK. Mr Traner is going to give Jo and me a ride home.'

'All right. Ring me if you need a ride, though.'

I kissed his cheek and dived from the car, starting

up the walk. And his car stayed where it was. My foot-steps echoed through my brain as I stared at the front door, growing larger and larger. *Dad, drive away, please!*

But he just sat there in the car, watching me. Oh, *god*, what was I going to do?

I didn't have a choice. I rang the bell and stood clenched on the front doorstep while it reverberated inside.

The door opened. Mrs Traner stood there, her dark hair gleaming in the light from the hallway. 'Oh! Hello, Emma.'

Behind me, I heard Dad drive away. My shoulders sagged. 'Hi, Mrs Traner.'

'Debbie's not here, I'm afraid; she's at the Sports Centre with her dad.'

'Oh! That's too bad – I mean, I just came by to – to get a book I lent her, but if she's not here, I can come back tomorrow, or – or maybe get it from her at school.' I backed away a step, clutching my bag and grinning in sheer relief.

Mrs Traner glanced up the street. It wasn't really dark yet, though the streetlights had come on. 'But wasn't that your dad who just dropped you off?'

'No, I took the bus. So, um – thanks anyway, Mrs Traner; I'll see you later.' Before she could say anything else, I turned and walked briskly up the street. When I was out of sight, I ran for the bus stop.

'Right, now that Emma's *finally* here, we can get started.' Sheila leaned across the dining table and tossed me a sheet of paper. 'This is the character you're playing,

OK, Emma? Usually you'd create one especially for you, but it takes a while, so we thought you could just play one of my old ones, from our last campaign.'

Everyone was eating pizza. I helped myself to a slice as I studied the sheet, which was broken up into dozens of categories like 'name', 'species', and so on. I was playing an elf called Tania, who was a rogue. That's the bit I could make out; the rest was in hieroglyphics.

Ski took out a plastic box of fluorescent green dice, and scattered them on the table. I stared as they clattered and bounced. They were all different shapes – a pyramid-dice with four sides, an almost-round one with twenty.

'Right,' he said quietly, flipping his blond hair out of his eyes. 'Who's ready to play Abby's game?'

Ski's low voice read the story to us, telling about the Evil Esmerelda, and how we had to save the Holy Eye. Then he took us into the dungeon, describing stairs and passageways and cold, bare walls. I listened intently, trying to see it in my mind.

'You're in a tunnel; it branches off to the left and to the right. To the right, there is only darkness. To the left, you hear the distant sound of maniacal laughter, and the echo of footsteps running away from you.'

'We'll follow the footsteps!' Sheila's pointed face was tense with concentration.

'OK. It's dark, you can't see anything.'

'I'll cast a light spell,' put in Rob.

'*You* can see anyway – you're an elf; you can see in the dark,' whispered Gail in my ear. I nodded, vaguely remembering something about that from the *New Player's Handbook*.

Sheila's mum came downstairs and poked her head in. 'Sheils, I'm going to the store, OK?'

Sheila gave her a wave without looking at her. A second later the front door closed.

Ski glanced down at Abby's game. 'OK, Rob – you cast light, and now you can see emptiness before you; a shadowy expanse stretching away into nothing . . . all is silent.'

Suddenly everyone seemed to be looking at me. I stared back at them. 'What?'

'You need to check for traps,' said Gail.

'Me?'

Rob nodded, taking another bite of pizza. 'You're the rogue; it's your skill.'

'Oh, right.' I rubbed my hands on my jeans under the table, trying to hide how nervous I was suddenly. 'OK, I'll go along the passageway and check for traps.'

'Roll a d-twenty,' said Ski.

What? I shook my head in confusion, but Sheila pressed a dice into my palm; the almost-round one.

I rubbed my thumb against the smooth plastic. 'Um, do I want high or low?'

'High,' said Rob and Gail together.

Ski nodded. 'You always want high.'

I rolled it, and it skittered across the table, landing with 19 facing up. The others whooped. Sheila craned her head to peer at my character sheet. 'And with your dexterity bonus, that's *twenty-three*,' she crowed.

Ski shoved his hair back. 'OK, you find a trap . . .
are you going to try to disable it?'

I nodded, and rolled again. I got a 17 that time.
So Tania was able to disable the trap, and the party
crept down the corridor, with the light from Rob's
spell flickering around us.

I could almost see the dungeon in my mind,
reflected in Ski's voice as he went on with the story.
And as he took us through the game's twists and turns
and secret rooms, the feeling that this place was
familiar came back to me again, stronger than ever.

Think, Emma, *think*! Secret rooms. A secret place.
Just do it like you do with Nat – close your eyes and
you'll be there . . .

Suddenly I saw Abby and me, studying the map of
secret places we made when we were nine. Running
to one of them, giggling and peering through the
fence at it.

'Hang on!' I didn't realize I had gasped it out loud
until the others stopped playing and stared at me.

'Emma, what is it?' Ski leaned forward across the
table.

My heart hammered so hard I could barely get the
words out. 'I just thought of something! I think I know
where Abby might have wanted to play this, where she
might have gone to set it up!'

'*Where?*' Sheila clutched my arm.

'That old house up the road, the one that's been
boarded up forever! It's just a few streets from here—'

Sheila's eyes grew wide. 'The one behind all the
trees?'

140

'Yes! We used to love that place when we were kids!' I jumped from my seat, grabbing my jacket. 'Come on, we have to go there!'

The old house was only a few streets away, hidden by a line of thin, dense evergreens. It was Georgian, I think. Really old, anyway, with half its shutters hanging off and all its windows boarded up.

It had been boarded up for as long as I could remember.

We used to go there a lot, Abby and me, and peer at it through the fence that stretched behind the trees. We could never quite get up the bottle to climb over the fence and explore the house close-up, but we used to make up all sorts of stories about it.

'It's haunted by a pale woman in white, whose husband killed her,' Abby would whisper, gripping my arm. 'He *cut her heart out,* and now she's condemned to wander across the rotting floors for all eternity, wailing . . . *wheerrre is my heeaaarrrt?*'

It's no wonder that we weren't that anxious to stroll around the place. But that was years ago. Who knew what Abby might do now?

A splintered hole gaped in the fence about a metre from the ground, making it easy enough to get a foothold and climb over, hidden by the trees. We sneaked around the back of the house, stumbling over bits of brick and rubble in the dark. There was a clattering noise as the shadowy bulk that was Gail tripped over something.

'*Ouch.* This is like being down a mine!'

'Hang on – I've got a torch on my key chain.' Rob

fumbled with his keys, and a small pinpoint of light appeared. It didn't help; it just made the darkness seem even darker.

A crumbling stone patio sat at the back of the house. The remains of a campfire were scorched in the middle of it, with empty lager cans lying everywhere. I licked my lips, and told myself there was safety in numbers.

'I can't see any way in.' Rob had been poking around the back door, which was locked and boarded up.

'What about over here, maybe?' said Ski. Kicking a lager can out of his way, he went over to one of the boarded-up windows. 'Or we could see inside, at least – this board is hanging half off . . .'

Rob joined him, stretching up on his toes and angling his torch against the window. A second later he dropped back down in frustration. 'It's too high up; I can't tell anything.'

'Lift me up, and I'll try,' I heard myself say. My voice actually sounded halfway calm, even though the thought of what I might see paralysed me.

Ski's eyes met mine as he turned around. 'Come on, then,' he said, holding his hand out. And even though Rob was taller, Ski was the one who lifted me, dipping his knees down so that he could wrap his arms around my thighs and heave me up.

All right, I admit it – my stomach swung a bit at the feel of his arms around me, and for a split second my brain raced along thinking inane thoughts like, *Would Dad really kill me if I had a boyfriend with a pierced eyebrow?* No, he'd probably just kill me if I had a boyfriend, full stop.

'Here, Emma, take this.' Rob pressed the little torch into my hand. I gripped the warm metal, and shoved away everything from my mind except what I was supposed to be doing.

The others clustered around Ski, staring up at me. Suddenly I felt almost nauseous with fear. Taking a shuddering breath, I shone the thin ray of light through the window. *Oh god, please don't let me see anything scary.*

At first, all I could make out were old boxes piled on grimy, bare floorboards. I panned the light slowly across the room, picking out tattered shreds of flowered wallpaper, a crumbling fireplace with a broken mantelpiece, pages of old newspapers.

And then I saw what was lying in the corner.

I screamed and dropped the torch, jerking back so violently that Ski almost fell over.

Pandemonium, with everyone screaming, 'What? What?' Somehow I was on the ground again, shrieking, 'Someone's in there! Lying in the corner, all huddled up – oh my god, it could be Abby, I think it's Abby! We have to get in there!'

I took in a quick glimpse of pale, frightened faces. No one was moving, no one was *doing* anything! Half sobbing, I tried to jump back onto the sill, churning my feet to get a grip. Someone pulled me back, and I staggered as I fell back onto the ground. Sheila.

'Emma, *wait*. Are you sure?'

'Yes! Someone's in there! We have to get *in*, don't you understand?'

'Oh, my god,' whimpered Gail. She pressed her fists to her mouth.

Ski gripped my shoulders, shaking me slightly. '*Listen!* If someone really is in there—'

I jerked away from him. 'There is! Look for yourself! Look!'

Ski's throat moved as he swallowed, glancing up at the window. 'Right . . . OK.'

So Rob lifted Ski up, and we all watched while he aimed the torch through the window. Sheila had her arm around my shoulders. I hugged myself, gripping my elbows with my fingernails. When I heard Ski gasp, I knew he had seen the same thing I had.

He looked ready to throw up when Rob lowered him back to the ground. 'Oh, god, I think you're right.' He ran a shaky hand through his hair. 'Um, right, I think we need to call the police. I mean, like, right now.'

Gail was shivering. 'Can't we go around to the front of the house first? I really don't want to stay here . . .'

Neither did anyone else. So we went back out to the street, picking our way through the wooded patch again and climbing over the fence. It wasn't nearly as easy this time; my hands could barely grip the wood. And then suddenly there were cars and lights and noise again, and I almost collapsed with the relief of it.

We stood clustered under an amber streetlight while I turned my mobile on. Right away I saw that there were about twelve missed calls from Dad. Which meant that I was in deeper trouble than I had ever even imagined before, but I couldn't think about it just then; I couldn't. I rang the police.

Of course I didn't have PC Lavine's card with me, though, so I had to ring 999. And it took ages to make them understand. I think at first the woman thought I was completely barking – she kept saying, 'Calm down, take a deep breath. You saw *what?*'

Finally I was able to explain what had happened in some sort of coherent fashion, and the woman said she'd send someone right away, and to stay where we were. Then she asked for my name. When I told her, there was a pause. I could hear the crisp tapping of a keyboard.

'Emma Townsend . . .' she repeated. 'Well, that's convenient – we had a missing persons report on you about an hour ago. You might want to ring your dad, love.'

So I had to think about it after all.

I practically got blasted off the phone at first. It turned out that Mrs Traner had rung him, and he had been driving around for the past two hours, trying to find me. He wasn't very happy about it.

I kept cringing, holding the phone away from my ear and saying, 'But Dad, *listen*—' while the others watched, looking worried and sympathetic.

Eventually I got through to him about Abby, and he went dead silent. 'Stay right there, I'm on my way,' he barked, and hung up.

The others took turns ringing their parents, too, telling them what was going on. Ski looked pale as he took out his mobile. 'I'm going to get bollocked for this,' he muttered as he sent a text. 'I'm supposed to be at home, being *responsible for myself* while Mum works the night shift.'

The police arrived first, but just barely.

I had thought that they might send PC Lavine and the other constable again, but instead it was two blokes, looking about seven feet tall as they got out of the squad car. I started to cry as I told them what I had seen; I couldn't help it. And then right in the middle of this, Dad's car screeched up to the kerb, parking crookedly behind the squad car. He hopped out with a face like a thundercloud about to split open.

'Emma, what's going on? What's this about finding Abby?'

Then Sheila's and Gail's mums arrived, and then Rob's dad, and everyone started babbling away at once. Finally it ended up with all the men going around to the back of the house while the rest of us waited on the pavement, our faces looking yellowish in the weird light. People passing by in cars kept staring at us. We must have looked like we were holding a convention.

Sheila's mum lit a cigarette, and blew the smoke up into the air, glancing at the house as if it were a snake about to strike. 'Right, tell us everything that happened again, *slowly.*'

Sheila took a breath. 'Well – you know how we play D&D—'

While Sheila tried to explain about live action role-playing, Ski's phone rang, and he stepped away from the others. I glanced after him, hoping he'd be OK.

'I don't understand this at all,' said Gail's mum flatly. 'Gail, you haven't told me about *any* of this, and now you—'

'Well, that's hardly the point now, is it?' said Sheila's mum, sucking on her cigarette. Her chin trembled. 'That poor girl . . . oh my god, I wonder what happened; I hate to even think about it . . .'

Gail's mum looked queasy. 'Well, we don't know anything yet. And Gail, look, you know it's just your safety I'm worried about, don't you? You can't just . . .'

Ski hung up and shoved his mobile in his jacket pocket. I hesitated, and then went over to him. 'What happened?' I whispered.

He snorted. 'Lots of hysteria about how could I do this to her . . . she's on her way now. Lucky me.'

A shaky laugh escaped from me. 'She sounds like my dad . . . he's going to *kill* me.'

Ski's green-blue eyes looked almost black in the light from the streetlamp. 'Yeah, snap . . . But you know what, Emma? It'll be worth it if we really have found Abby. I mean, even if she's . . .' he trailed off, obviously remembering what we had seen.

'I know.' My stupid eyes started leaking again, and I looked down, swiping at them with my hand.

Ski touched my arm. 'Emma, it'll be OK . . . don't cry.' He dropped his hand and shoved his fists in his pockets.

I nodded, groping for a tissue in my pocket and wiping my nose. Part of me really wanted him to hold my hand or something, which must have made me the most terrible person in existence. I mean, how could I have even been *thinking* of that then, of all times?

'They're coming!' called Rob suddenly.

Everyone snapped around. The police were emerging from around the side of the crumbling house, with Dad following them and Rob's dad behind.

'Curtains,' said one of the police officers as he joined us on the pavement.

We all stared at him.

He brushed at a smear of dust on his shirt as he elaborated. 'Some old curtains, rolled up and thrown in the corner . . . mind you, it really did look like a person at first; we had to break in and go have a look to be sure.'

The second police officer opened the door of the squad car and leaned in, doing something with the radio.

'Aye, I'm not surprised you thought it was a person . . . there was a bit of mildew that looked just like hair, from a distance. But listen, you lot.' He straightened up and looked at us, his eyes serious.

'You were right to ring us, but you shouldn't have been nosing around back there in the first place; it's dangerous. Not to mention that it was trespassing – that's an offence, you know. We could press charges against you for it.'

He scanned his gaze over us, and nodded slightly, apparently satisfied by our stricken faces. 'We'll leave you to your parents to sort out, but I don't want to hear anything from you lot again, all right?'

Curtains. I couldn't look at anyone, couldn't say anything.

We hadn't found Abby after all.

* * *

'What concerns me most is that you don't seem to understand how serious this is.' Dad spoke in this quiet, spookily controlled voice, like tidal waves of rage were just barely being held back. He was sitting in my desk chair while I cringed on my bed, staring at the carpet.

'No, I understand,' I managed. 'But—'

He sliced at the air like he was karate-chopping a fly. I gulped, and shut up.

Dad stared at me, tapping a pen against my desk. 'You lied to us about where you were going. Again, after promising me just yesterday that you could be trusted. Now, what am I supposed to do? Eh?'

If I moved, I would shatter into a million pieces.

'*Trespassing*. Do you have any idea how serious this is? Anything could have happened to you. Anything! Besides which, it's illegal – and who are these kids you're running around with now, anyway?'

'Just – friends of Abby's.' And of mine, maybe.

'Emma, I don't like it. I don't know anything about them, other than that they apparently encourage you to lie to us, and trespass—'

'That's not fair!'

He took a deep breath, and threw the pen down. 'Look – I know you've been upset about Abby. It's incredibly upsetting, for all of us. But I won't have you going out of control, lying to us – Jenny thinks that I shouldn't punish you, but I don't agree; I think you need to realize how serious this was—'

'I *know* how serious it was!' I yelled. 'We were trying to find Abby! Nothing's more serious than that!'

The rafters shook as Dad bellowed, 'That's not for you to do! That's the police's job, do you understand?'

'Yes, but—'

'No!' Dad stood up. '*Not another word*, Emma. I mean it!'

'But Dad – please listen, OK?' I spoke in a rush, frantic to get the words out before he started shouting again. 'It's just that we realized where Abby might have been setting up a live action game when she disappeared, and—'

'Emma, stop it! You're not a detective! This isn't a game! If you keep on like this you're going to get hurt, or cause the police even more trouble. Now, quit mucking about in police business!' He jabbed his finger in my face. 'Do you understand? That's *final*.'

I stared at my duvet cover, struggling not to cry.

Dad's face looked like he had just bitten into one of the super-hot peppers that Jenny grows. 'Right, I hate to do this, but you're going to have to stay at home until you prove you can be trusted again. You're not to go anywhere, do you understand? Not without my express permission.'

Express permission. Does that mean I get it quickly? 'For how long?' I muttered, wiping my nose with the corner of my pillow.

'Until I say.' And he left, banging the door shut behind him.

I sat hunched on the edge of the bed, hugging myself. All around me, my posters stared down at me from the walls, mocking me. Stupid, insipid posters of actors and pop stars who I didn't even like.

Suddenly I hurled myself off the bed and lunged at the walls, ripping the posters off, tearing the glossy paper to shreds and yanking flakes of paint along with the Blu-tac. I didn't stop until my walls were almost bare. Becks survived, and one or two others, but that was all.

Next I turned to my wardrobe, flinging open the doors. Shoving aside the pile of old clothes and cuddly toys, I dragged out the cardboard box and sank down next to it, surrounded by scraps of poster.

Slowly, I prised open its flaps. There they were – books upon books, most of them with the spines broken from having been read a thousand times.

Emma, you've got to read this – it's utterly fantastic.

Oh, it's by Tanith Lee! I love her stuff!

Books with bright pictures of dragons on the covers, of spaceships, of strange planets. I piled them carefully on the carpet, arranging them by author and stopping to read bits here and there. I realised I was smiling, a broad, soppy grin. It felt like they had been in exile, and now I had them back.

And then I got to the bottom of the box, and my hand slowed down.

My notebooks.

I hesitated, wondering if I really wanted to go there. It was enough that I had my books back, wasn't it?

Finally I reached in to pull one out – and then dropped that one to dig even deeper, until I found the one with the blue-jean pattern on its front cover. PROPERTY OF EMMA L TOWNSEND, proclaimed red paint-pen in big letters. I used to sign everything 'Emma L'.

151

The L's for Louise, which I hate, but I thought 'Emma L' sounded cool.

Almost dreading what I would see, I opened the notebook and started to read. The green-inked words were both familiar and strange.

The two novice mages had been travelling for many days, seeking the evil enchantress Esmerelda in her kingdom of Colldara . . .

But I couldn't read the words without hearing Karen's voice. Nausea dipped through me. I started to shove it back into the wardrobe – and then stopped.

Karen wasn't even *here*, and I was still scared of her! What was I scared of? A memory? Setting my jaw, I opened the notebook again. And as I read, I began to relax, caught up in the wonder of my own words. At some point I moved into the bed, snuggling under the duvet, turning pages. I kept reading until I got to the last page.

I couldn't read that one because it had been torn out, leaving only a few bits of paper clinging to the spiral binding.

Day Thirteen

... Yet Abby's parents say they have not given up hope. 'I try ringing her mobile almost every hour,' said Mrs Ryzner. 'And I know Greg and Matthew, our sons, keep trying to text her ... I just can't stop thinking that maybe one time she'll pick up.'
The Daily Post, Friday 17th September.

Jenny drove me to school that morning. We didn't say much. Well, it would have been difficult anyway, what with Nat's favourite kiddie CD blaring away, and Nat herself yodelling along in the back seat.

As we inched through the sticky traffic near St Seb's, Jenny turned the volume down. 'Emma, listen – I've mentioned to your dad that maybe counselling might be a good idea for you.'

Here it was, then. I stiffened, not looking at her.

'You seem really upset about Abby, that's all.' She darted a glance at me. 'Going off without telling us, and what you did to your room last night—'

'It's my room,' I muttered.

'Well, I just think, and your mum agrees, that maybe

153

it's all got to be a bit too much for you, and—'

I whirled around in my seat. 'You spoke to *Mum* about this?'

Jenny's voice stayed level. 'Yes, we spoke last night once your dad got home with you. She's very worried about you, Emma, and so are your dad and I.'

I was actually trembling, I was so angry. 'What, do you think I'm insane, then? Why? Because I want to find Abby? Because I took my posters down? Ooh, yes, call the loony bin!' In the back seat, Nat had fallen silent, staring at me with wide eyes.

Jenny manoeuvred the car around a lorry that was signalling left. 'Emma, come on . . . that's not what counselling is about. It's very helpful to get your feelings sorted when you're a bit confused, that's all.'

I gritted my teeth as I glared out the window at the passing houses. Damn Jenny, anyway. And Mum. All of them holding secret conferences about me, deciding they knew what was best.

We pulled up to the school. Jenny's blue eyes rested on me, worried. 'Emma, we just—'

'I'm not confused,' I told her. And I grabbed my bag and shoved open the car door, slamming it shut behind me.

I was, though, to be honest. Confused, I mean. I kept thinking about Ski lifting me up to the window, and the pale, huddled figure I had seen. I had been so certain it was Abby – and it was just curtains. Squares of stupid cloth used to cover windows. Then my thoughts would drift to Ski again, and guilt would stab me that I was even thinking about him, that I could actually like a boy in the midst of all this.

At lunchtime I sat by myself in the noisy canteen, trying to finish a worksheet for History. As though I actually cared about the struggles of the suffragettes. It wasn't like I got a vote at home.

Looking over my shoulder, I saw Jo and Debbie sitting over by the vending machines. Debbie was showing something to Jo, who had her chair balanced on its front two legs as she craned forward to look.

Were they texting Karen again? My stomach jerked, and I looked down hastily, staring at the worksheet. Doodling a triangle in the margin, I thought about the pages and pages of the story I had read through last night, and wondered if I'd ever have another best friend. A real best friend, someone who I didn't have to pretend with, or worry that she'd turn against me.

Stop it! I glanced at question five and wrote the first rubbish that came to mind, my jaw clenched tightly.

Dinner that evening was stiff and stilted, with Jenny trying to pretend everything was wonderful, and Dad hardly talking to me. As soon as I could, I escaped to my room and put a CD on. I should have been doing my maths homework, but I totally wasn't in the mood. Instead, I flopped onto the bed with one of my newly-liberated books.

My mobile rang before I had read a page. 'Just thought I'd tell you what happened after you left last night,' said Sheila's voice.

155

'What?' Glancing at the door to make sure it was closed, I slid down onto the floor, crouching on the opposite side of the bed.

'Well, once we got home after carrying out your brainy idea, Mum rang the police and spoke to PC Morton. You know, the one who was with PC Lavine?'

'And?'

'And they had already searched the house, OK? They searched it when Abby first went missing, and then *again* after we went and talked to PC Lavine. They've been checking out all the empty buildings or whatever where Abby might have gone to set up a game. There's nothing there. There's nothing anywhere.'

My heart plummeted. I swallowed hard, running my finger along the skirting board. 'Oh. Oh, well, at least we tried.'

'I *knew* it was a stupid idea to go barging over to that old house! I should have listened to myself!'

The back of my nose prickled. I sniffed and said hastily, 'Um . . . were things OK with Ski's mum last night?'

'No, not really. She turned up just after you left with your dad . . . she's always pretty hysterical anyway, but she really outdid herself, screaming and crying. The police took *ages* to calm her down and make her realize that we weren't all being arrested. Ski looked like he wanted to sink into the ground.'

I was silent for a second, taking in the information that Sheila seemed to know Ski's mum. I played with a corner of the duvet. 'So . . . is he OK?'

'He seemed OK at school today. A bit hacked off.'

Did he say anything else about me, though? My mouth went dry. Like an idiot, I parroted again, 'So, um, he's really OK?'

There was a pause.

'Do you want his *number*, so you can ring and make sure?' sneered Sheila.

My cheeks burst into flames. Thank god she couldn't see me. 'Sure, why not?' I said, totally offhand, like I rang boys all the time. As if I'd actually be brave enough!

When we hung up, I sat beside the bed for a long time, staring at the wall.

Nothing found anywhere. Nothing.

That night I dreamed that Abby and I were walking through the woods, dressed in grey cloaks with wrought-iron flowers at our throats. All around us, the forest leaves shone like stained glass in the sunlight.

Abby gave me an impish smile. 'Do you remember Esmerelda?'

My veins chilled. 'Yes, of course.'

'Well, it's really important for you to find her.'

I wanted to shout, *No!* I barely managed a groan, clutching my pillow, trying to fight my way out of the dream.

The forest shifted, and we were in a glade drenched with sunlight. Abby's hair poured down to her waist in a chocolate river, glistening with warm highlights.

She held the tiger-eye necklace. It shone brown and gold in the sun, winking at me.

She draped it around my neck with royal formality, and then fluffed my hair out from under its chain. 'Keep it safe,' she murmured, touching the stone as it lay on my chest. 'It's yours now.'

'Abby – Abby, please don't go.' I grabbed her hands, holding them tightly in my own.

She smiled sadly. 'I have to, Emma. But keep looking for Esmerelda, OK? It's all down to you, you're the only one who knows. Promise me.'

'Yes – yes, OK, I promise.' The wind murmured through the grass, and the sunshine sparked Abby's eyes, so alive and warm and brown, and I thought – *this isn't a dream.*

Abby kissed my cheek, her lips as light as a butterfly brushing past. 'Goodbye, Emma,' she whispered.

I came slowly awake, my pillow damp with tears. My stomach ached like someone had kicked me with a steel-tipped boot. It had been so *real* . . .

The warm shape at my feet shifted as Pippin rose and stretched. He picked his way across the duvet to me, and butted my chin with his head. I scooped him into my arms, burying my face in his fur.

'Oh, Pippin . . . it was like she was really there . . .'

I was going mad; I had to talk to someone. The dream was like Abby saying, *Don't give up.* But I didn't have a clue where to start, what to do!

I sat huddled up, rocking slightly, trying to think. Finally I opened the drawer and took out the little dragon, clutching him with his wings jabbing against my palm. A place with passageways, stairs, secret rooms . . . come *on,* Abby! Where were you going? Tell me!

Pippin blinked at me, his paws tucked cosily under his orange-striped body.

He looked blissfully unconcerned that I was losing my mind.

Day Fourteen

Even though it was only Saturday, Dad insisted on doing his special brunch again, first rattling around in the kitchen for ages and then finally sweeping in and putting croissants with ham and cheese on the coffee table. '*Et voilà! Le petit déjeuner extraordinaire!*'

Jenny smiled at him as she pressed down the plunger on the cafetiere. 'Mmm . . . looks good.'

'Yum!' said Nat.

Dad kissed the side of Jenny's head. '*Bien sûr, ma chérie,*' he said, practically gurgling the words with his phoney French accent.

I sat in the armchair, apart from everyone, and picked at my croissant. It was flaking crumbs everywhere, and I pressed them against the beige fabric, watching tiny grease stains appear.

'Shall we go do something this afternoon?' said Jenny. 'Nat, watch your crumbs; you're getting them all over the carpet.'

Dad shook his head. 'I've got that management training thing at two o'clock, remember? Over at the Reading office.'

Wonderful. He could learn how to be even bossier.

I tuned them out, frowning down at my half-eaten croissant. *Passageways, stairs, secret rooms . . . stairs, secret rooms, passageways . . .*

'Does that sound OK, Emma?' asked Jenny.

I glanced up. 'What?'

Jenny sat curled up in the corner of the sofa with her coffee, smiling hesitantly at me. She opened her mouth to reply, but Dad jumped in first. 'Jenny was just explaining that we might be able to get you a counselling appointment next week.'

My vision actually went red for a second. I had thought that was just a saying. I stood up and shoved my plate onto the wooden tray. 'I've already told you, I'm not going.'

His mouth tightened. 'Emma . . .'

'Dad, if you'd just *listen* to me—'

He leaned forward, his black-haired forearms resting on his thighs. 'I *am* listening. But your mother and Jenny and I have discussed it, and it's what we've all agreed is best for you. We're concerned about you, love.'

'But—'

'Emma, come on. Enough, OK?'

I started to slam out of the room. Dad's voice stopped me. 'And take your things to the kitchen, if you've finished.'

I grabbed up my plate and my empty coffee cup, and resisted the urge to throw them both at him, splattering his pristine chinos and polo shirt. Stalking to the kitchen, I rinsed off the plate and cup and shoved them onto the draining board.

Voices drifted in from the front room, and my hands slowed as I strained to listen. *I'm sure it's the right thing . . . really difficult for everyone . . . just give her time . . .*

'Emma?' Nat had followed me into the kitchen.

'Shh!' But Dad had put the TV on, and now all I could hear was a sport's commentator enthusing away about a perfect pitch. I sighed, and looked down at Nat. 'What?'

She leaned against the counter, the top of her curly head barely reaching over it. 'Can we play today? You said we'd finish before, and we never did. I want to know what happens to Esmerelda.'

I stared at her. 'Yeah . . . that's a good idea,' I said slowly. 'I want to know, too. We'll play right after Dad leaves, OK?'

Nat gave a little hop, bouncing on her toes. 'Why not now?'

'Because it's a secret,' I whispered, glancing towards the front room.

Dad left about an hour later, clutching the briefcase that seemed to be welded to his hand sometimes. The moment he was gone, Nat and I went out into the garden to sit under the birch tree. Pippin padded after us and stretched out on the grass, rolling on his back in the sunshine.

'We were consulting with the mages of Ganet,' prompted Nat, eyes shining.

'Right.' I looked up at the softly rustling leaves for a second, thinking. 'Well . . . the mages are very old and wise, and they tell us what we need to know. Esmerelda and Jasmine have joined forces, and they've fled to – to the castle of Colldara.'

'Where's that?' Nat's expression was grave, searching.

'Far away, but the mages have a magic mirror we can walk through that will take us there. But we have to hurry, Nat! Esmerelda and Jasmine have stolen something called the Holy Eye – that's this beautiful necklace, with a stone like the eye of a tiger. It has great powers, and we can't let them use it, or they'll destroy the world.'

As well as I could from memory, I plunged into the story Abby had written. And Nat and I entered Esmerelda's dungeon, two apprentice mages who were in way over their heads. My voice lowered as I described the dungeon's twists and turns, its passageways.

'Are you there?' I whispered. 'Do you see it?'

Nat's hair bounced on her shoulders as she nodded. Leaf-shaped shadows from the tree fell across her face.

My hands were tight fists. 'Right, now – I want you to think a minute, OK? If we were going to chase Esmerelda through these dungeons for real – I mean, act the game out for real . . . where would we go to do it?'

Nat's eyes flew open, and she scowled at me. 'That's not part of the game!'

I crouched on my knees beside her. 'It *is*, Nat. Honestly. Come on, where do you think we'd go?'

'A big basement somewhere,' she said dismissively.

'Now come on, she's getting away!' I slumped back onto my heels, disappointment swelling through me. *Stupid!* Had I actually thought this would work?

The back door slid open, and Jenny stuck her head out. 'I'm making brownies,' she called up to us. 'Fancy helping?'

'We're busy playing!' called back Nat. I winced. God, that was all Jenny needed to hear! She'd probably be on the phone to my *counsellor* any second now.

But Jenny just laughed, and pulled out a blue ceramic bowl from behind her back. 'Are you sure? I've got a bowl here with your name on it – lots of ooey, gooey chocolate.'

So much for Esmerelda. Bouncing up with a squeal, Nat sprinted for the door. I sighed and started to stand up – just in time to see her stumble over a tree root and go flying. A second later she lay howling on the grass.

Jenny dropped the bowl with a clatter, and we both ran for her. She was clutching her arm, sobbing, and I saw that she had smashed it against one of the rocks that bordered the flowerbed. It was already ballooning up, the skin tight and angry.

'Mummy, I hurt it, I hurt it!'

'You sure did,' murmured Jenny, white-faced. She put her arm around Nat and carefully helped her up. 'Right, let's get you to the hospital . . . we need to get that X-rayed. Emma, you'll be OK here?'

I nodded, and stooped down to peer into Nat's face. 'Listen, Natty, don't cry – if you've broken it, they'll give you a really trendy cast, and I'll sign it when you get back, OK?'

Nat nodded, trying to look brave but failing. Jenny slowly ushered her through the house and into the car, and a few seconds later I heard them drive off.

I drifted back into the house and cleaned up the chocolate that had splattered on the carpet, rubbing at the stains with a damp cloth. A big basement . . . I sighed and dropped the cloth into the bowl. Thanks, Nat, that's just hugely helpful.

I went to dump the bowl in the kitchen, and as I was washing my hands, the memory hit me full-blast. I stared out the window with the water still running over my hands.

'Oh, my god . . .' I whispered.

It was at the Family Fun Fayre. The last one we went to before we started secondary school at Balden, and everything went so wrong.

We had been playing the Esmerelda game, poking around the empty office buildings. And afterwards, we had run down an embankment to the outside fence of the plant, and started following it around, heading back to the Fun Fayre. It had been a scorching day, and I remember Abby heaving out a sigh, blowing a strand of black hair off her face. 'The heat is a device of Esmerelda's, no doubt.'

The fence curved around the plant, and suddenly there was a large garden shed in front of us, built against the side of the slope.

'Hey, what's this?' Abby went up to the door. The

sign on it said RESTRICTED ACCESS, but the knob turned when Abby put her hand on it. She creaked open the door and peered inside. 'Emma, come see!'

I glanced around, but there was no one to catch us nosing about. The fence was set back a little ways from the road, with a small wood shielding us on the other side.

So I moved through the long grass to join Abby at the shed, looking over her shoulder, and felt coolness brush against my skin. A cement floor, and stairs that led downwards, disappearing into a tight, close darkness.

'What do you think?' Abby had whispered, her brown eyes gleaming. 'Shall we risk it for a biscuit?'

My heart pummelled as I turned off the water. We had only gone down there for a few seconds, just long enough to make out concrete corridors lined with dozens of pipes. We didn't have a torch, so we couldn't explore it properly. And anyway, I think we were both too scared.

But maybe Abby had taken a torch and checked it out for herself at the next Family Fun Fayre.

Maybe she had even found a way to get into the plant.

I clutched the edge of the sink, head wheeling. Sheila! I had to talk to Sheila! I dashed to my room, scooping up my mobile and dialling her number.

It rang about ten times, and then kicked into her voice-mail. 'Sheila, it's Emma! Ring me as soon as you get this, *please* – it's really, really important!' Then I rang Directory Enquiries and got her home number, and stood tapping my fist against my bureau as it rang.

No answer.

Maybe they weren't even home. Maybe she hadn't even taken her mobile with her, wherever she was! My message could be sitting in her room for hours, waiting. And I didn't have hours. If Abby were down there—

I burrowed frantically in my bag for PC Lavine's card. I had this moment of panic where I thought I had lost it, and then found it tucked into my wallet.

Her mobile clicked into voice-mail instantly. 'Hello, this is Police Constable Elizabeth Lavine. Please leave a message, and I'll ring you back as soon as possible. If this is urgent, please ring Hampshire Police Department on . . .'

'Um, hi,' I said when I heard the beep of the voice-mail. 'This is Emma Townsend. I need you to ring me, please – it's really important, I think I might know where Abby went.'

My voice sounded strangled. Just for good measure, I rang the number for the Hampshire Police, too. A woman's voice answered.

'Hello – um – may I speak to PC Lavine, please?'

'What is this regarding?' She sounded brusque, like I was her zillionth call of the day.

'Just – I need to talk to her. Is she there, please?'

'I'm sorry, I need to know what this is regarding.'

'Please, can I just—'

'PC Lavine isn't in today,' broke in the bored voice. 'Can I direct your call somewhere else?'

I hung up without thinking and stood there shaking, pressing my hands against my head. What was I going to do? Abby could be down there right now! She could have fallen and hurt herself—'

Ski! I fumbled with the mobile's keyboard, punching in his name from my address book. It rang three times. Five.

'Hello?'

'Ski, it's Emma!' I blurted. 'You've got to help me, I think I know where she might be—'

'What?' Ski's voice cracked, suddenly sounding deeper. 'Emma, what is it?'

I told him everything, and when I finished, there was a long pause.

'Well? What do you think?'

'Um . . . I don't know. I mean, I wouldn't be in a hurry to call the police out on another wild goose chase, if I were you.'

'I'm not!'

'Could you tell your parents?'

'No! My stepmother's at the hospital, and my dad's at some conference, I don't even know where – Ski, what if she's *down* there? She's been gone – she's been gone just two weeks, so she could still be alive, couldn't she?'

He sounded miserable. 'Emma, I don't know. I mean, yeah, it sounds possible, but . . .' he trailed off. 'Couldn't you wait until PC Lavine gets back?'

'I don't know! I left her a message, but she's not even *in* today – what if she doesn't get it until Monday?'

'Or talk to someone else there—'

'*Who?* The one who thinks she was doing drugs, or the ones who caught us trespassing?'

'Yeah, but Emma, come on, they'd still go check it out—'

'But they might not do it fast enough!' I shrieked at him. 'They might think it's just us being stupid again! Ski, Abby could be down there! She could be hurt! We have to go there now, we have to go see—'

Ski's voice turned higher again. 'Go there? How will you get in? There's a fence, right?'

'I don't know! If there's not a way in, then it's not where she went, is it?'

He didn't say anything.

'So – are you coming, or not?' I gripped my phone so hard I thought I might break it.

'Emma – oh, shit. Look, I'm really sorry, but I can't, OK? My mum – god, I'm already in so much trouble—'

'I'm in trouble too!' I snapped at him. 'Do you think you're the only one? My dad's going to *kill* me! But I have to do this for Abby; I don't have a choice—'

Tears choked my chest. Suddenly I was sick of talking to him, sick of hearing his bleating excuses. I hung up on him, and then ran downstairs to the kitchen, rooting about in the utility drawer. Grabbing the torch, I turned it on briefly to check that it had batteries, and then shoved it in my back pocket.

Snatching my house keys from my jacket pocket in the hallway, I stopped to scribble a quick note:

Jenny,

I'm really sorry, but I had to go check on something very

important. I'll be back later this afternoon. I'll be OK, I promise. Please, PLEASE don't tell Dad!!

Emma x

I left the note on the fridge, under Jenny's magnet that said LIFE'S TOO SHORT TO ENJOY BAD WINE. A thought struck me, and I dashed upstairs to grab the dragon, shoving it deep into my pocket for luck. Stupidly, it made me feel braver. Now I wasn't completely alone.

I ran out the back door, locking it behind me.

I wrestled my bike out of the garden shed, struggling to extract it from the lawn mower. It wobbled a bit when I got on, but a moment later I was out of the alleyway and onto the main road, cycling towards Clarkson Chemical Plant.

The plant was on an industrial estate about a mile from where we used to live. I stopped in front of the main fence, propping my weight on one leg. The grounds spread before me like a green carpet, with the gleaming main building reflecting clouds and sky. There were hardly any cars in the parking lot.

I kicked off and started heading around the left-hand side of the building, where I remembered the shed being. Slowly, the view behind the fence gave way to industrial chimneys and barrack-like buildings.

I came to the patch of woods and stopped, peering through the thick foilage. I couldn't see anything, so I pulled my bike off the road, leaning it against a tree, and walked towards the fence. The undergrowth grabbed at my legs with every step.

Before I got there, I could see the shed, just a few

metres further down on the other side. Right. Now, how could she have got in?

The answer was right in front of me.

I took a step backwards, scanning the top of the fence as far as I could in both directions. There weren't any security cameras that I could see. Not that that meant anything; maybe they were just out of sight, watching my every move.

Hesitantly, I touched the chain link fence, half expecting an electric shock, or for an alarm to go off. But nothing happened, and after a moment, I took a deep breath and started to climb.

The worst bit was as I swung myself over and started climbing down the other side. I was positive that sirens were going to start wailing, and that men with dogs would erupt from over the hill, barking and shouting at me.

But nothing happened. Dropping awkwardly to the ground, I walked over to the shed.

The door swung open when I turned the handle, and I stepped inside to the same dark coolness I remembered from before. In the middle of the floor, the stairs plunged downwards, waiting. I wiped my hands on my jeans, trying to get the nerve up to go down them.

Suddenly I froze. I heard someone stumble, and swear. The crunching sound of footsteps was coming from the woods.

My heart felt like a bird that might die of fright. I yanked the torch out of my back pocket. A completely pitiful weapon, but it was all I had. I pressed against the wooden wall, clutching the torch and praying that whoever it was wouldn't see me.

The crunching noise stopped. Silence.

'Emma?' hissed a voice.

Ski!

I burst out of the shed. He stood on the other side of the fence, wearing black jeans and a black T-shirt with a wolf on it. His shoulders relaxed when he saw me. 'Hi.'

'Hi.' I walked slowly over, and we stood facing each other with chain link between us, like Visitor's Day at the prison. 'You said you weren't coming.'

'Yeah, well . . .' He sighed, shoving his hair back. 'I wasn't going to, but I couldn't let you do it alone. Pretty stupid, huh?'

I thought it was pretty wonderful, actually. I glanced past him into the woods, and saw my bike, along with another one, propped against a tree. 'Is that your bike?'

'Yeah . . . I saw your bike from the road. I brought them both into the woods so no one else would notice them.' He glanced up at the fence. 'Right, um – how do I get in? Just climb?'

I nodded. 'Yeah . . . I don't think there are any security cameras around.'

Ski smiled slightly. 'Well, that's good. Always useful when there aren't any security cameras.'

He jumped onto the fence; it shook and rattled as he climbed up it. He paused for a second at the top, adjusting his hands around the naked edges of the chain link, and then threw his leg over and backed down the other side.

He dropped to the ground with about a metre to go. I cleared my throat and pointed to the shed. 'That's it.'

Ski shoved his hands in his pockets as we walked over to it, but sort of jumped forward to hold the door open for me as we went in. I turned my torch on, and shone it down the stairs. Ski crouched on his heels, staring downwards. A tangle of pipes at about head-level burst into view, and a passageway.

'How far does it go?' he asked.

'I don't know . . . if it goes all under the plant, it could go for miles, practically. And there's more than one passage; Abby and I saw that much when we went down.'

'Just like the scenario,' murmured Ski. Neither of us said anything for a moment, and then Ski cleared his throat. 'I brought it, by the way . . . Abby's game. If she meant for it to be played here, then maybe we can follow it, like a map.'

Prickles burst over me. Following Abby's game without her here, and not knowing what we'd find . . . I swallowed, and nodded.

Ski pulled a torch from the waistband of his jeans, and gave me a weak grin. 'Right – let's get this over with.'

We climbed to the bottom of the stairs, the light from our torches kicking with every step. The darkness swallowed us.

'Wow,' whispered Ski, shining the torch around him. 'What a great place to play live action.'

A concrete tunnel ran in front of us, for as far as

our torches could make out. Two more branched off from it, one on each side. Pipes of all different sizes ran everywhere – above our heads, along the sides of the walls. A faint droning noise hummed through the air.

Reaching into his back pocket, Ski pulled out some folded-up pieces of paper and shone his torch on them. 'Right, um . . . the first thing that happens in Abby's game is that we hear the maniacal laughter, and footsteps running off to the left.'

I went first, clutching my torch. It was much, much darker once you got away from the bottom of the stairs. There was no light at all – just our torches, which seemed laughably feeble.

I struggled to keep my hand steady as we moved forward, terrified that I might suddenly see a face or something, looming towards us out of the darkness.

'Don't forget to check for traps,' whispered Ski.

'What?'

'Traps – remember when we played the game? She probably would have set some up for real, for us to find.'

A loud hissing split the air, and I started as my heart tried to jump from my chest. Ski froze at my side. Seconds passed with nothing else happening, and I was just about to relax when a gurgling noise erupted, bubbling and echoing.

'It's just a pipe,' I squeaked.

Ski let out a breath. 'Yeah.'

We started walking again. Ski's shoulder brushed against mine in the narrow space. I was so incredibly glad he was there. I couldn't imagine pacing through this darkness alone.

Actually, I could. It was beyond horrible.

After what felt like around twenty minutes, we came to a T-junction, with pipes snaking off in every direction. A cluster of them plunged into a wide, dark hole against the wall.

Ski went to the edge of the hole and shone his light into it, and then took out the pages again. 'Right . . . um, according to the game, here's what happens now.' He read by the light of his torch.

As you come to a crossroads, you hear a clanging sound. A wall has sealed off the passageway behind you. There is no way through it. Suddenly a silky female voice splits the air: 'Greetings, foolish mortals! I am Esmerelda, and this is my dungeon. You're all certain to die, but I think I'll play with you first. You may go either left or right. One way is instant death, the other, life . . . for now.

My palms turned to ice. I was afraid to turn around, afraid I'd actually see the wall. 'Didn't – didn't we go right when we played it at Sheila's house?'

Ski's shadowy face grimaced. 'Yeah, but the thing is, it doesn't matter. All she's got written here is, *Whichever way the party goes, they hear Esmerelda say, 'Congratulations! You've chosen life.'* Then take them to the first dungeon area.'

'Where's . . . the first dungeon area?'

He jammed the pages back in his pocket. 'I don't know. The tunnels must connect at some point, but Abby's the only one who knows where we're meant to go from here. Fun, eh?' He gave me a half-hearted grin. 'Left or right?'

I stared into the darkness. 'Right, I guess.'

The pipes ran in a thick tangle along the ceiling. The air felt damp, and I shivered in my T-shirt. We came to another T-junction and went right again. This tunnel turned out to be endless, and we crept down it for what seemed like hours, trying not to stumble over odd bits of pipe lying about.

'Emma, I think we've gone the wrong way.' Ski had the sheets out, flipping through them. 'We should have found some traps by now, and some rooms – all sorts of stuff.'

'Should we go back?' We were both whispering. It was hard not to, in the dark.

'Yeah, I think we have to . . . only maybe we should just go left at that last T-junction, instead of going all the way back to the first one. If the tunnels all connect, we've as much chance of finding something there, don't you think?'

'God, don't ask me!'

We retraced our steps, which seemed to take hours, and finally got back to the T-junction. The left-hand passage stretched before us, just as dark and endless as the last one.

Suddenly I noticed my torch. Instead of casting a strong, round light, it was more like a halo with a dark centre.

I jiggled it. 'Ski, my torch is going!'

'We've got mine.'

My chest went cold, clutching at me. 'But what if yours goes too?'

'It won't. I mean, it shouldn't.' An edge of doubt crept into Ski's voice, and we stared at each other.

'Come on,' he said finally.

Hundreds of footsteps later, we came to another T-junction.

'Um . . . should we go back?' I was trying very hard not to panic.

Ski licked his lips. 'I don't know . . . we've come so far already. Maybe . . . maybe if we just keep going, we'll find something.'

So we went along that tunnel for ages, and then it branched off again. And then again. I could hardly see now, and I stumbled as we picked our way over a scattering of loose pipes. 'Ouch!'

Ski was at my side instantly, his face dipped with strange shadows. 'Are you OK?'

'Yeah . . . but my light is almost gone. Look at it!' I was near tears as I shook it. It flickered a last time, and went dark.

'Hey, come on – it's OK, we'll both use mine.' Ski hesitated, and then his hand found mine and closed around it, firm and warm, and we kept going.

And I would be completely lying if I said that I was only thinking of finding Abby right then. My heart was slamming against my ribs so hard it hurt, and for a moment all I could think of was whether my palm was sweaty or not.

'How long have we been down here?' whispered Ski after a while.

I shook my head. 'I'm not wearing my watch. Maybe a couple of hours?'

'That's what I thought.'

'We're – we're lost, aren't we?'

'Um . . . well, I think I know how to get back to where we started, sort of . . . the thing is, it would take so long now that I'm afraid *my* torch might go out.'

'But if we get lost, someone would find us, wouldn't they?' I wasn't able to keep my voice from shaking.

'I don't know,' said Ski. 'Why would they come down here unless they needed to check the pipes? As long as the pipes are OK, I bet they don't even bother.'

'Well . . . well, even if your torch went out, we could find our way back. We'd just have to feel our way along the walls.' Brave words! Icicles jabbed my stomach at the thought of it.

Ski let out a breath. 'Let's talk about something else, OK?'

Don't panic. Think calming thoughts. 'Yeah, OK. What?'

'Um . . . I don't know.' After a pause, he said, 'Why don't you tell me what happened between you and Abby?'

I could only make out the barest outline of his face. 'Me and Abby?'

'Yeah. I mean, I only have Sheila's version . . . I'd like to hear yours.'

So I told him. About going to Balden in Year Seven, and Abby's pretend games. How I had been so embarrassed by her, and started avoiding her – but hadn't wanted to hurt her feelings, so had pretended everything was all right.

'And . . . there was this group of girls led by Karen Stipp, and I really – really admired them, I guess.

And in October, a Saturday dance club started up at the Arts Centre, and Karen and the others were joining – so I decided to join too, to try to be friends with them, and then Abby heard about it, and *she* joined.' I went silent, remembering the utter torture of it.

'Let me guess,' said Ski. 'Disaster.'

'Yeah, in one . . . She had just started getting into Goth, and she'd wear these weird outfits to the Arts Centre. And that was it. Karen and the others started in on her at school, calling her Goth Girl, only Abby didn't even care. And when they saw they couldn't get to her, they started in on *me.'*

I kicked at a fragment of loose concrete, sending it skittering across the dark tunnel. 'So, um – they started really picking on me. I mean, non-stop, for the rest of the year. They used to call me Freak, and – all gang up on me with it. They had half the year hating me in a few months.'

Ski's hand tightened. 'That's awful.'

'It was nothing compared to – to this one time. That was the worst, the absolute worst.' My throat clutched up.

Ski was silent, waiting. I was so thankful for the darkness. I could never have told him, or *anyone*, about this in the light.

'See – see, Karen and I had PE together, and – there was this one time when I had just got out of the shower, and – she had taken my clothes. And my towel. And – and no one would give them to me.'

My throat felt too small. I stopped, waiting to see

if Ski would laugh. He didn't. 'And meanwhile, Karen had got hold of my notebook, and was reading this story I had written out loud.'

'And then – wait for it, kiddies – the evilll Esmerellllda turrrrrned and growled, "I'll have you both thrown in the dungeon for this!" Ooh, stop it, mummy, I'm scared!'

Karen had cooed and gurgled her way through my story, capering around the changing-room, waving my clothes in the air with one hand and clutching my notebook in the other. Everyone was in hysterics. I mean, complete hysterics – weak-kneed, hanging onto each other and howling with laughter.

I huddled against the lockers, wet and naked as my own words attacked me. Trying to cover myself, wanting to die.

'Emma, the famous writer!' shrieked one girl.

'Freaky L. Freak – ohmigod, look at her!'

Finally, Karen had thrown my clothes back at me. 'Here you go, Freak – cover yourself up before we're all sick. But I'll keep this last page, it's just so-o good. Hey, will you sign it for me?' She ripped it out of the notebook. 'No? God, what are you crying for? Never mind, I'll get rid of it—'

She ripped it up and flushed it down the loo, laughing about how it was just like loo roll.

Our footsteps echoed down the dark corridor, and I realised that for the first time, I could think about that day without crying. 'You know what?' I said softly.

'I think I hated Karen the most for making me hate my story.'

'I'd feel the same way. She sounds completely evil.'

'But *you* wouldn't have let her get to you!'

He glanced at me in the dim light. 'Wanna bet?'

'But – Ski, come on! I mean, you have a pierced eyebrow, and go to Wilkinson!'

Surprised laughter burst out of him. 'Emma, I only have a pierced eyebrow because I knew it would irritate my mother, OK? And Wilkinson's not that different from other schools . . . you still have people who think they're better than anyone else.'

We came to another T-junction and looked at each other. Finally we went right again.

I let out a breath. 'Anyway, it had been terrible all year, but that was – that was the worst. So that afternoon I went home and asked Dad if I could change schools in Year Eight.'

'I don't blame you.'

'But, Ski, the worst part is that I actually – sort of hated Abby by then. I felt like if she had just tried to fit in more, none of it would have happened. And then when I changed schools . . . I just ended it with her. Didn't answer her phone calls or anything. And I wish—'

I couldn't speak for a second. I swallowed hard, and swiped my hand over my eyes. 'There's just . . . there's just no one else like her.' I whispered.

Ski glanced at me. His hand gripped mine tightly, and we walked along in silence.

All at once the tunnel opened out into a large four-way crossroads, with a sort of open room at the middle, and pipes shooting in all directions. Ski shone his torch around. A faint drumming sound came from the pipes.

He pulled out the pages again. 'Um . . . would you say this is the heart of the dungeon?'

I stared at him. 'Why?'

'Because if it is, then we're back on track – Abby mentions it; there's a sort of riddle we're meant to solve here.'

'*What?*' I leapt beside him, peering over his shoulder.

His fingers clutched the paper, creasing it as he pointed. 'Here—'

As the heart of the dungeon draws nigh, you must follow the blue arrow as it flies – to be led to your goal, if you still think it wise.

The torch's light moved as he turned the page. 'Only . . . it doesn't give the answer.'

'A blue arrow,' I murmured, gazing at the darkness around us.

'She must have drawn one somewhere!' Turning in a frenzied circle, Ski shone his torch about the walls and floor, sweeping it in great arcs. Bare concrete, grey walls. 'Nothing! Damn it, there's *nothing!*'

Suddenly I remembered the dragon, and I shoved my hand in my pocket and gripped it. Just close your eyes, concentrate . . . what would Abby and I have done in the game? The tiny wings seemed to move as they pricked my palm, and I gasped, almost dropping it. And then Abby stood in the glade again, smiling at me.

Two novice mages. *The blue arrow as it flies* . . .

My eyes flew open. 'Ski, give me the torch!' Grabbing it from him, I shone it at the ceiling. And just as if I had known it all along, I saw that the pipes had coloured arrows on them.

The one with blue arrows shot across the ceiling, heading off into a tunnel to our left. Our footsteps pounded as we followed it, the torch bobbing wildly.

'Ski, look!' I clutched at his arm, pulling us both to a halt.

Just ahead, a thin length of string had been stretched across the tunnel at ankle level.

'A trap,' whispered Ski.

I ran towards the string, clambering over a cluster of pipes to crouch down in front of it. The trap had been tied around a pipe at each side of the tunnel. I touched it gently, plucking it like a guitar string, unable to speak.

Ski knelt beside me. 'Oh, god, she was here; she really was . . .'

He took the torch from me and shone it down the passageway. 'Look, there are other traps . . . this is where she meant for the game to be played.'

'It's where she meant for it to end,' I said softly. Because I had just seen what was hanging up on the wall.

The tiger-eye necklace, dangling from a bolt on a pipe. It burst into brilliance as Ski directed the light onto it, and I heard him suck in a quick breath.

I rose slowly, gazing at the faint winking of the stone, remembering the light in Abby's eyes as she showed it to me on the bus. Tiger-eye, for courage . . . Swallowing against the dry lump in my throat, I took another step forward, reaching for the necklace.

'Emma, no!'

The light wrenched away from the stone as Ski lunged for me, tackling me around the waist. A scream ripped from me as we fell to the concrete floor together, hard, Ski's elbow jabbing me in the stomach. The torch rolled across the floor, plunging us into darkness.

I lay there gasping, trying to get my breath back. Ski scrambled up. 'Oh, god, Emma, are you OK? I'm sorry, I didn't mean to hurt you . . .'

'I'm OK,' I gulped. 'What—'

Ski had crawled after the torch. 'Listen,' he choked out as he turned to the last page. '*As you reach for the Eye, a noise erupts, and a chasm opens beneath you. Try for it if you will.*'

With a shaking hand, he shone the light at the base of the pipes. My stomach lurched as I saw the gaping hole in the floor that they ran into.

A half-empty bottle of Pepsi lay beside the hole. There was a dried puddle of spilled cola next to it.

Ski's voice was ragged. 'She must have – Emma, when she put the necklace there, she must have—'

He didn't finish. On my hands and knees, I moved towards him and took the torch. Crawling back to the hole, I closed my eyes for a moment, trembling.

And then shone the light into the hole.

The heavy pipes fell downwards, plunging at least ten feet to another layer of concrete and pipes. The light wasn't strong enough to make out much, but what I did see froze my heart.

Abby's battered grey rucksack, lying on the floor with its contents scattered.

By the time Ski and I finally made it back to the entrance, his torch had started fading, and it turned out we had been in there for over four hours. I was so shaky by then I could hardly even climb the stairs, and Ski wasn't doing much better. I think we were both in shock, or something. Plus I was so thirsty I thought I was going to faint.

We rang the police as soon as our mobiles got a signal. PC Lavine had been trying to ring me, it turned out; she had got my message after all.

Then I rang home.

Dad was there, and I started crying as soon as he answered the phone. I could hardly get the words out to tell him what we had seen. 'Shh, it's all right, love,' he soothed. 'Start slowly, tell me what's wrong . . .'

For once – for once – he actually listened to me. And when he turned up about half an hour later, and found Ski and me sitting together at the top of the cement steps – Ski with his arm around me because I had been crying – he just sat down with us and listened to all we had to say.

It seemed like a miracle.

The police had already arrived by then, delving into the tunnels with some workers from the plant, who had turned the lights on. As we sat waiting for them to come out, I told Dad everything, gasping the words out against my tears.

'Dad, I'm sorry – I know I shouldn't have trespassed . . . I was just so afraid that – that she was down here, and no one knew, and she might be – hurt.'

His eyes had turned bright when I told him about the rucksack, and now he hugged me, pressing me against him. Neither of us said anything for a long time. Finally he pulled away, and looked me in the eyes.

'Emma, I'm sorry; I should have listened to you more. I was just – well, it was – difficult, thinking of what might have happened to Abby, and I was worried about you . . .' A muscle beside his mouth moved. 'I hope you can forgive me.'

I couldn't speak. I nodded and threw myself against him, and we hugged tightly. (Forgetting all about poor Ski, who sat there probably melting with embarrassment.)

As though thinking the same thing, Dad pulled away from me and held out a hand to Ski, leaning across me. 'We haven't been introduced properly,' he said gruffly. 'I'm Emma's dad, Tom Townsend.'

Ski's face was pale, with smudges of dirt all over it. He straightened up a bit, and shook Dad's hand. 'I'm John Kazinski . . . Ski.'

Dad glanced at the tunnels, and let out a breath. 'Well . . . thank you for taking care of my daughter, Ski. When I think what could have happened to the two of you in there . . .'

Ski shook his head. 'She didn't need me to take care of her. She's the one who had the guts to actually . . . to actually look down the hole.'

None of said anything after that; we just sat pressed together on the stairs until the police emerged, about twenty minutes later.

And even though I had already known, in my heart, that Abby was dead . . . I guess there had still been a tiny glimmer of hope, because we all jumped up when we saw them, and my heart pounded so hard that it hurt.

But their faces said it all.

After

There was a huge press explosion once it came out how Abby had been found, with screaming headlines everywhere: *TEEN HEROES FIND ABBY.* It was horrible. I wasn't a hero; neither was Ski.

Thankfully, Dad had a long talk with my form head and Mrs Ottawa, so that when I went back to St Seb's, everyone pretty much left me alone. It was a massive relief. I couldn't have handled it if everyone at school had treated me like a hero, too.

Instead, when I walked in on my first day back, I saw a tall blond girl and a short dark-haired one waiting by the trophy case. And it was almost like none of it had ever happened.

I hesitated, and then walked over to them. Jo touched my arm, smiling uncertainly. 'Ems, are you OK?'

I lowered my bag to the floor, engrossing myself with pushing it flush against the wall. 'Yeah, I guess.'

'It's so . . . so amazing what you did,' said Debbie. 'You and that boy, John.'

I saw Abby's knapsack again, lying on the cold,

hard concrete. I folded my arms over my chest. 'He's, um . . . called Ski. And – look, not to be rude, but I don't want to talk about it, OK?'

A steady stream of people passed by the trophy case as they came into school, staring at us and then quickly away. Debbie tossed her dark, wavy hair. 'Fine. Anyway, we've got a bone to pick with you.'

'Yeah.' Jo's gaze narrowed a bit.

I stared at them both, blood hammering at my temples. Freak. Freak. This was it, they were going to say it, they were going to tell everyone.

And suddenly I realized that I didn't care if they did. *I didn't care.* Glorious freedom swooped through me. It wasn't just that I had Sheila and Ski and the others for friends now – I just didn't care, full stop. No one could ever make me feel like a freak again. Not ever.

I lifted my chin. 'What bone?'

Jo tucked a strand of blond hair behind her ear. 'Listen, you, why didn't you tell us that Karen Stipp's a total bitch?'

Eh? My mouth dropped open. 'But you – you liked her so much in the café, and you've been texting her – I heard you texting her, talking about *pretty freaky*!'

Jo's expression melted. 'Oh, Ems . . . We were just responding to something *she* said! That was before she told us what it actually meant.'

Debbie's eyes snapped angrily. 'Yeah, she said some really awful things, Ems.'

I was silent for a minute. 'But . . . what if everything she said was true?'

'What do you mean?' demanded Debbie.

190

I lifted my chin. 'Well, what if that thing really *did* happen in the changing rooms – I'm sure she told you about that little incident, right? – and what if everyone *did* call me a freak, and totally shunned me, and—'

Jo shook her head impatiently. 'I didn't say we didn't believe her, just that she's an utter bitch! God, the way she treated you at Balden – and then to laugh about it to us, like we'd think she was really clever or something!' She shuddered.

Tears jumped to my eyes. 'I thought—'

'You thought we'd dump you if we knew,' said Debbie in a low voice. 'Ems, how could you? We're your friends.'

'But you didn't even notice how upset I was at the café! Why didn't—'

'Ems, of course we noticed!' Jo looked shocked. 'Only we thought it was *Abby* you were upset about; we couldn't figure out what we had done!'

'No offence, but we can't read your mind,' said Debbie. '*You* were nice to Karen; how were we supposed to know?'

I looked at the gleaming rows of trophies in the case, and then back at them. 'OK . . . but what if my Darth Vader clock *isn't* post-ironic? And what if I like shopping in the Dungeon, and – and all sorts of stuff that I was too embarrassed to tell you about?'

Debbie propped a shoulder against the wall. 'You mean all that fantasy stuff that Karen said? It's no big deal, Ems. I mean, I like to sew; *that's* hardly the epitome of cool.'

'Hey, we don't care if you're weird,' laughed Jo. 'We just want you to talk to us again.'

'Yeah, and besides, you still have to help me win the fashion contest,' said Debbie with a grin. 'Don't think you get out of it that easily.'

I did start to cry then, even though I felt so stupid doing it – in the middle of the foyer, with everyone watching! The three of us hugged each other, laughing.

I thought fleetingly of Karen, and almost felt sorry for her.

Not quite, though.

I rang Mum the day after we found Abby. This time I was going to forget about being polite or shy or whatever, and just tell her to come – but I didn't have to say anything at all once she heard what had happened. She started to cry, and said that she'd book a flight that same day.

Jenny and I went to meet her at the airport a few days later. We waited with the rest of the crowd behind the railings, and finally Mum emerged after getting through customs, looking slightly bedraggled from the flight and wheeling her black suitcase behind her. She dropped it when she saw me, and we hugged for a long time.

When she stepped back from me, she said, 'Emma, you've grown . . .'

I wiped my eyes, laughing. 'I'm the same height as I was!'

She smiled. Her own eyes were bright. 'Yes, I

suppose you are. But you've grown just the same, haven't you?'

At the inquest, the pathologist testified that Abby had died instantly when she fell, hitting her head against a gasket on one of the pipes. 'She probably literally never knew what happened; she wouldn't have felt any pain.' He was a dark-skinned man with thick black hair, and kind eyes.

His gaze rested briefly on Abby's parents, who sat together in the front row, holding hands. 'I can assure you that from the head wound she sustained,' he repeated softly. 'Death would have been instantaneous, with no pain.'

Watching from where I sat between Mum and Dad, I saw Abby's mother let out a shaking breath, closing her eyes. Mr Ryzner put his arm around her, hugging her against him.

Ski and I both had to testify, too. I saw him sitting with his mother across the courtroom, looking totally unlike himself in a pair of dress trousers and a white button-down shirt. As the coroner called my name, he caught my eye and gave me a tiny smile.

I was terrified that I'd break down and sob, or garble the details or something, but it was all right. I kept my gaze on my parents as I answered the coroner's questions, and their eyes encouraged me as I explained how I had known about the tunnel, and what made me realize Abby might have gone there.

I didn't mention anything about the dream, though, with Abby standing in the glade of sunshine.

Or the dragon. They were too private, nothing to do with anyone but me.

After everyone had testified, the coroner gave his verdict: death by accident or misadventure. Misadventure. What a stupid word, like she just barely missed having loads of fun.

But at least it was over. The courtroom filled with rustling and talking as everyone stood up, starting to file out.

'Wait a minute,' I said to Mum. 'I just—' I swallowed. 'I want to say something to Mr and Mrs Ryzner.'

They stood talking with some of their neighbours who had come. I went up and touched Mrs Ryzner's arm. A cascade of emotions flowed over her plump face as she turned and saw me. 'Emma . . .'

'Mrs Ryzner, I just wanted to say – that I'm sorry.' I gripped my handbag, digging my fingers into the leather. 'I mean, sorry that I stopped being Abby's friend. I was stupid, and – and I really miss her.'

Her face startled to crumple as I spoke, and suddenly she was hugging me. I clutched her tightly, breathing in the smell of her linen blazer.

'Oh, Emma, darling, don't apologize . . . I know you always loved her, deep down. And – how can we thank you for finding her?' She dabbed a tissue against her eyes. 'What we imagined was so very much worse.'

Ducking her head down, she put the tissue away in her handbag. When her eyes met mine again, she tried to smile. 'Emma . . . I wonder if you'd say a few words at Abby's funeral?'

And though my throat was like sandpaper, I felt a tendril of warmth spread through me.

'I'll try,' I whispered.

A few days before Abby's funeral, I sat at my desk, struggling to write. I had already scratched out pages of clumsy attempts, and the one I was working on now didn't seem much better. I didn't even know what I wanted to say. I slumped on my hand, staring down at the messy scribbles on the page.

My thoughts drifted to Ski. We were planning on going to the park the Saturday after Abby's funeral with Sheila and the others, to plant an oak tree in her name. And he wanted to take me to a movie next week – there was a new science-fiction film that we both wanted to see. Smiling slightly, I doodled the planet Saturn with a spaceship flying past it.

Behind me, Nat sat on my bed, looking through the D&D book and whispering a story to herself. A cast encased her broken arm, covered in colourful grafitti.

'Emma, can we play Esmerelda later?'

My shoulders tensed. I never wanted to play that game again.

'No . . . No, I think Esmerelda is gone now, Nat. But we'll play a new game, OK? You can make it up yourself, and tell it to me.'

Her eyes lit up. 'And we'll both play it?'

'Sure.'

Dad came in then, leaning against the doorway. 'Nat, go help Mummy in the kitchen, would you? I want to talk to Emma for a minute.'

She bounced off the bed. 'Emma, can it be about bears? Wizard bears?'

I grinned at her. 'Wizard bears sound seriously cool.'

As Nat skipped out, Dad came in and stood beside me. And just as I glanced up at him, he gently laid my blue-jean patterned notebook on the desk.

I gaped at it, and then up at him.

He sat down on the edge of the desk, shoving his hands in his pockets. 'Emma, I have to confess . . . when you were gone that Saturday, and we didn't know where you were, Jenny and I searched your room to see if we could get any sort of clue. And I found this.'

'Did you *read* it?' I pulled it towards me defensively.

Dad nodded. 'I'm sorry. I thought – I don't know what I thought. That you were getting involved in something bad, or – I don't know.'

'I wrote this *two years* ago!'

He looked sheepish. 'I figured that out after I read a bit, and to tell you the truth, I would have put it back sooner, except—' he smiled. 'Well, I got too inter-ested in the story to put it back.'

I couldn't speak for a minute. 'What – really?'

'Yes, really. I had no idea you were so talented – that you have such an amazing imagination.'

Heat crept up my face. 'It wasn't all me. Abby and I both thought up the story.'

'But you're the one who put the words on the page. You have a real way with words, Emma. I felt like I was part of the story.'

'So you don't think I'm *odd?*' It was out before I could stop myself.

'Wha-at?' Dad's eyebrows shot up. 'Emma, of course not! You like a lot of things that *I* don't necessarily like—' he motioned around my room, which now had some of its starship and fantasy posters reinstated (along with gorgeous Becks, of course) – 'but that's just you, isn't it? And I'm very proud of who you are.'

'So . . . um, what about counselling, then?'

Dad smiled ruefully, and rubbed at the dark stubble on his chin. 'Well, I think what I said in the first place was good advice, actually, if I had just followed it myself . . . we should be OK so long as we talk to each other. Only this time, I promise that I'll listen to you more. How does that sound?'

A warm glow filled my chest. 'It sounds good,' I whispered.

Looking almost as embarrassed as I felt, Dad cleared his throat and motioned to my scribbled sheets of paper. 'Anyway, how's it going?'

I showed him all the scratched-over bits. 'I can't work out what I want to say, or how to say it.'

He squeezed my shoulder. 'Just tell them about Abby.'

As I stood at the lectern, I pressed my hands against it to keep them from trembling. The scent of flowers filled the air. The church was a solid sea of faces, all turned up towards me, waiting.

I licked my lips, and started to read.

'I want to tell you about a girl called Abby. She was my best friend for most of my life, and I had some really wonderful times with her . . .'

I spiralled back to the very beginning and told them about Esmerelda, and being novice sorcerers together. About laughing in the Wendy House in her back garden, and teasing her twin brothers until they ran in to tell her mum. About spending the night at her house and inventing perfect worlds where unicorns could swim in the sea.

About being friends.

'Abby believed in magic.' I gripped the paper as my voice echoed through the church, amplified through the microphone. 'She taught me to believe in it, too. Even though she's gone, that part of her will always be with me. And I'll always remember her for that.'

I could hear people crying as I finished reading. I wiped my eyes with a tissue, and said, 'Thank you for letting me tell you about her.'

I went back to my seat, where Mum, Dad and Jenny were waiting for me, and cried for the rest of the service.

After the funeral, I tried to give Mrs Ryzner back the dragon I had taken, but she wouldn't let me. 'You keep it, Emma.' She closed my fingers around it. 'It can help you keep hold of that magic you talked about.'

So it sits on my bedside table now, the last gift I ever got from Abby.

Except that wasn't true. She had given me myself. I knew now that I wasn't just Emma, or Ems – they were both a part of me. Ems with her streaked hair and trendy clothes. Emma's dreaminess, her writing and pretend games. The way Ems managed to laugh at everything, and be popular. They were both me.

I touched the dragon, tracing the coil of its serpentine neck.

'Thanks, mate,' I whispered.